Bea Is for Blended

ALSO BY LINDSEY STODDARD

Just Like Jackie

Right as Rain

Brave Like That

Bea IS FOR Blended

LINDSEY STODDARD

HARPER

An Imprint of HarperCollins*Publishers*

Library of Congress Cataloging-in-Publication Data

Names: Stoddard, Lindsey, author.

Title: Bea is for blended / Lindsey Stoddard.

Description: First edition. | New York, NY : Harper, 2021. | Audience: Ages 8-12. |
    Audience: Grades 4-6. | Summary: Soon after her mother marries a man with
    three sons, sixth-grader Bea Embers fights to form a girls' soccer team at school,
    despite discrimination and setbacks.

Identifiers: LCCN 2020035149 | ISBN 978-0-06-287816-8 (hardcover)

Subjects: CYAC: Stepfamilies—Fiction. | Soccer—Fiction. | Sexism—Fiction. |
    Middle schools—Fiction. | Schools—Fiction. | Moving, Household—Fiction.

Classification: LCC PZ7.1.S7525 Be 2021 | DDC [Fic]—dc23

LC record available at https://lccn.loc.gov/2020035149

Typography by Sarah Nichole Kaufman

21 22 23 24 25   PC/LSCH   10 9 8 7 6 5 4 3 2 1

First Edition

For my mom and dad,
For loving me up to the Care Bears.

1

MOM MAKES ME PROMISE I won't bicker with Bryce today. So even though I caught him sneaking pepperoni off the platter before the ceremony, messing up the pattern of slices, I don't say anything. There's greasy evidence smudged on his rented tuxedo shirt, but I bite my tongue in the back of my mouth and remember how Mom looked right in my eyes and said, "Please, Bea. Not today," and how I looked right back in her eyes and said, "I got this."

My aunt Tam is reading a poem about new beginnings that makes me want to gag, and there are sixty-two people staring up at us with teary eyes. This isn't a new beginning, I think. It's a disastrous end.

At least I don't have to wear a dress or worry about

matching anybody else, because I'm the only one on this side. On my mom's side.

Opposite me, Cameron and Tucker and Bryce stand with their hands behind their backs. They match. Gray suits and blue bow ties. Bryce catches my eye and smirks and smacks his lips in a way that says I-know-you-know-about-the-pepperoni-but-you-can't-say-anything *so ha*. I squeeze both fists around the thick sunflower stems, and even though I want to blow the whistle, hold up a red card, and point him to the bench, today I just have to let the ball roll. Because today, my mom is marrying his dad.

I close my eyes when Wendell and my mom kiss, and open them when Wendell snorts. He always snorts when he happy-cries, and it'll be a while before he can stop. It's the same snort he has for sappy movie endings and those news stories when military parents come home and surprise their kids at school. It's the same snort that came from the way back of the gym during our end-of-year banquet, when Coach Wright talked about the importance of teamwork and how both coed rec teams had an incredible year of working together.

Wendell couldn't quit the snorting so he stepped out through the gym's double doors. I rolled my eyes at Nelle and Fern, the other two girls on my team, and Wendell missed when I got called up to receive the league's Most

Valuable Girl award. And when Bryce got Most Valuable Player.

Coach Wright handed us the awards and we had to stand next to each other so they could take a picture for the local paper. Nelle and Fern gave me little half smiles and I ran my fingers over the trophy. It was smaller than Bryce's. Everyone applauded but I knew what they were thinking. They were thinking I was more valuable than Bryce, and they were right, because I scored more goals, had more assists, and never got tired or needed a sub like he did. But, they were thinking, at least she got something.

Most Valuable Girl.

My eyes burned when I held the award and I wished Mom hadn't been called for an emergency at work because she would have stood up and said that this is *some bullsharky*. But I'll tell you one thing. I didn't cry. I bit my tongue in the back of my mouth and didn't smile for the camera.

I threw the trophy in the big black garbage bin on the way out.

The officiant announces that my mom and Wendell are married and Mom sends me a little smile because during the rehearsal last night she told him very clearly he was not to say *man and wife*. "We are man and woman, or husband and wife, but we are not *man and*

3

wife," she said. The officiant nodded and made a note in his folder, and Mom crossed her arms over her chest and leaned into me for a secret Embers-girls fist bump.

At least she's not changing her name to Valentine. That is the last name on Earth to suit her, all heart-shaped and construction-paper pink. Even Wendell agrees that she's an Embers for life, bright and sparky and ready to ignite. And that's me too.

The organ player starts an upbeat song that fills the chapel and everyone stands and claps. Wendell pulls Cameron and Tucker and Bryce into a big Valentine hug and I can hear him whisper, "I love you boys so much." Then he puts his hand on my shoulder and smiles and hugs me too. He and Mom walk hand in hand down the three steps toward the aisle. Mom leans over to hug Grandma Bea in the front row and Wendell starts snorting again and wipes tears from his face. That makes Mom and Grandma Bea share a little Embers-girls laugh, not a laugh-at-him kind of laugh, but an oh-Wendell-you're-sappy-but-we-love-you-anyway kind of laugh.

Mom leans into him and they start walking again. She's wearing a small sunflower in her dark braid and her dress is ivory and flowy and falls easily over the curve of her belly.

That curve is the reason for all this. They were going to wait at least until Cameron and Tucker went to college. There was no rush, they kept telling us. They were going to keep taking it slow.

But now there will be another kid.

And I wonder which side that kid would be standing on if it were here. I wonder if it'll be a Valentine or an Embers.

Wendell kisses the top of Mom's head and puts his hand gently on her back. His finger has a new ring on it. It's different than the ring he was wearing the day he met my mom, the ring he just stopped wearing five years ago, the ring he keeps, with another ring, in a tiny blue porcelain container on his kitchen windowsill.

I watch his hand rub a small circle on my mom's back and my eyes burn, but then the officiant gestures for Cameron and Tucker. They throw their arms around each other's shoulders and move together down the aisle behind Mom and Wendell, waving to family in the first row. Everyone smiles at them in their matching suits and bow ties. Then the officiant signals to Bryce and me.

We step forward and meet in the middle, him in his gray suit and blue bow tie, me in my black swishy pants and red top, red like the US Women's National Team away jersey, red like embers. But I stay tight to my side of the aisle and hold the sunflowers between us. We are not on the same team, and he is not about to put his greasy pepperoni hand over my shoulder, even if the officiant told us it would be nice for the camera. No way.

Mom and Wendell have their first dance and everyone circles around with champagne glasses in their hands. I'm standing between Grandma Bea and Aunt Tam and the photographer squats in front of us and changes the lens on her camera. Then flash! Flash! Flash! Flash! A hundred little clicks make Mom and Wendell glow and they're laughing at something that exists only in the little space between them. And I wonder if it's their new baby. The only one of us who is both of theirs.

Then the music changes from slow and sappy to fast and dancy and Wendell is opening his arms and waving us all to join in. Aunt Tam is first. She hollers *whoohoo!* and pumps her arms to the beat, and then Tucker bounds into the circle and starts playing an air piano, his fingers moving up and down the pretend keys, and before I can think of how to get out of this I'm being nudged out to dance too.

Grandma Bea holds both my hands and knows all the words. *Ain't no mountain high enough!* She swings my arms and it makes me move my feet and my pants swish around my ankles. I don't really know how to dance, but I'm good at soccer moves, so I pretend there's a ball on the floor and do a couple of step-over-scissor fakes. Grandma smiles big and sings, *To keep me from gettin' to you, babe!* She's belting the song right to me and I don't mind that so much because it's better than looking at everyone twirling and mixing all over the dance floor.

This is exactly what Mom wanted. All this mixing. "No sides of the chapel," she told the wedding planner. "No seating chart. Just let everyone blend." She smiled up at Wendell when she said that last part. Bryce rolled his eyes and I did too and I think it was the first time we agreed on something.

As Grandma spins me around and sings at the top of her lungs about high mountains and wide rivers I'm thinking that's what people call us now. Blended. Except my side didn't get to add as much to the mix. It's been my mom and me from the very beginning. Now it's my mom and me and Wendell and Cameron and Tucker and Bryce. Plus, they have two dogs and one cat, Dodger and Roscoe and Fred. It doesn't seem fair, us adding two and them adding seven. Like the ref should blow his whistle and call a foul. *Too many players on the field!*

And I'll tell you one thing. If I got to choose one to send to the sideline, it'd be Bryce. I like him even less than the cat.

2

I DON'T UNDERSTAND WHY it's called a honeymoon. Mom never lets anyone call her honey, and they're not going to the moon. They're just driving to the Champlain Islands for two nights. But I wish they actually would go all the way to the moon, and stay awhile, because as soon as they get back Mom and I have to tape up our last boxes and leave the condo so we can move into a new house with enough space to blend.

I don't like sharing. Not one bit. And even though I don't have to share a bedroom in the new house, I have to share all the other rooms. It's bad enough already because Bryce has my same birthday and every year they make an announcement over the loudspeaker at school. *And a very happy birthday to Bea Embers and*

Bryce Valentine. And in fourth grade, when kids found out my mom was dating his dad, they started calling us The Twins. But I'll tell you one thing. I'm exactly six hours older than Bryce Valentine and I am not sharing any blended birthday parties with him. Ever.

When I wake up, I can hear Grandma Bea in our kitchen and I hope she's making pancakes. Hers are the best. Plus, whenever Mom is gone and Grandma sleeps over she adds M&M's to my breakfast because she knows they're my favorite and she gives me a wink like this is something we don't have to tell Mom. And I nod and smile, because even though I'm not one for secrets, this is one I'll keep.

I open my bedroom door and peek down the hall. Grandma's whisking batter at the counter. "Morning, Bea," she calls.

"Morning," I say and slide onto my stool. We only have two stools in the kitchen because we only need two, and I like it that way.

"I still just wish Mom would—"

"Bea," Grandma cuts me off fast and turns around with a dripping whisk. "Three."

I know I'm not getting around Grandma Bea's threes this morning. No one ever does. My mom did them every morning growing up, reciting three things she was grateful for before Grandma let her get out of bed, and that's how Mom has always woken me up too. *Good morning, Bea. What're your three?*

"Big or small," Grandma says. She pulls a pack of M&M's from the pocket of her apron, and gives me a little wink. "Three things."

I take a deep breath and think about the yard sale Mom and I found last week. "One, cleats that fit. Two, the soccer net for our new yard. And three . . . M&M's."

Grandma Bea spreads a ladle of batter on the griddle then looks me right in the eyes and says, "Those are good ones."

And that's the thing about Grandma Bea's threes. It's kind of like a time-out huddle. You might be down 2–0 with one minute left on the clock but a good captain reminds you of what you *do* have—like the best speed on the field, a strong left foot, or a secret weapon flip throw-in when you get within striking distance of the goal. And Grandma's a good captain.

She pours out five more pancakes and waves me over to drop in the M&M's. I make my soccer number, ten, on each one and Grandma grabs a spatula from the drawer. "Now, what were you saying about your mom?"

And that's the other thing about Grandma. She's good at reminding me that I have a lot to be grateful for, but she still listens to what's making me feel cruddy. Even lucky kids go through hard stuff, she says.

"I still don't understand why we can't stay in the condo. Mom and Wendell could just keep visiting each other." My M&M tens are getting all rainbow-melty. "The baby could stay with us, I guess. Or we could switch at halftime, when it turns nine or something."

Grandma chuckles a little and flips the pancakes. "I hear you," she says. "It'll be hard at first." She turns down the griddle and points her spatula at me. "But Wendell is good. And so are those boys." I want to tell her that she doesn't know Bryce and how he acts when he's around Kenny and Morris, but before I can, she says, "Your mom is happy."

I roll my eyes and Grandma rolls hers right along with me and says, "Oh, I know. It's total hogwash and Wendell's ruining everything."

I smile. "Exactly."

She pulls out two plates and slides three pancakes on each, then puts the jug of maple syrup on the counter, pours two glasses of milk, and sits down across from me on the other stool.

"Mmmmmmm," she hums after the first bite. "I love when your mom is out of town." That gets us both laughing and Grandma's laughs are like Wendell's snorts. They're hard to stop once they get started.

We blow bubbles in our cups and get enormous milk mustaches and eat with our fingers and talk with our mouths full and when we're done we leave the dishes in the sink and Grandma pulls me into her apron. "If you ever get sick of those boys and need some elbow room, you know what to do." I'm thinking she's going to say I can come visit her any time, but instead she juts her elbow hard like she's sinking it into Bryce's ribs and says, "Take it."

Then she gives me a look that says *you got this*.

Grandma's phone rings and she doesn't even say hello when she picks up, just, "You're not supposed to be worrying about anything, remember?" Then she pulls the phone away from her ear and mimics Mom blabbing. We snicker and I'm thinking Mom will ask to talk to me so I put my hand out for the phone and act like I'm annoyed even though I'm not because I kind of miss her too. But Grandma says, "OK, Louise. We will. Now go have fun."

She hangs up and says, "She wants us to go check on the boys. Make sure they're not running circles around their grandmother who is way, way older than I am." Grandma smiles and unties her apron and puts her hand on my shoulder. "Come on now, Bea, let's go make sure Grandma Ethel is still kicking."

I'm feeling like a starter who's been benched, and going to check on whether the Valentine boys are playing fair is the very last thing I want to do. But then Grandma says, "We'll stop on the way home for ice cream, because

we're going to need some dessert after that breakfast."
Like I said, Grandma Bea's a good captain.

On the way to the Valentines' house, Grandma says, "Let's take a detour down your new road," and turns right onto Evergreen. It's dirt, like most of the other roads in our town, but not like the condo that is walking distance from the village. The houses on Evergreen all have an upstairs, and garages for two cars, and front and back and side yards with trees separating them onto their own land. Even though we only live two roads over, it doesn't feel anything like this.

Our condo has one floor, and two bedrooms, and we share a carport and a wall with Aunt Tam. We share a yard with her too, and our back decks touch so she can just step over to our ours anytime and she knows how to let herself in. And even though I'm not one for sharing, I don't mind sharing with Aunt Tam. We moved into the condo when I was two weeks old so Mom and Tam have been friends my whole life.

Mom likes to remind me that as a baby I would cry and cry for what seemed like forever, like double overtime into penalty kicks, without quitting. "Always had that fire in you," she tells me. "You're an Embers all right."

On our first night in the condo, I cried and cried and nothing was working so Mom wrapped me in a blanket and walked outside in the cold Vermont air until my cries turned to whimpers and humming snores that sent little white puffs to warm the space between us.

And when I was sleeping like that, she tiptoed toward the back door and opened it to go inside, but I woke and cried, so she started over, walking the yard again, bouncing and shushing.

Then the light next door turned on and Tam shuffled out to the yard in her bathrobe and winter hat and big boots. Mom whispered she was so sorry and how embarrassing to meet our new neighbor this way, but Tam shushed my mom and put her arm around her shoulders and walked the yard with us. They took turns holding me, and running inside to make hot chocolate, circling the yard while I slept. And when the sun came up, Aunt Tam pushed my blanket down below my eyes and said, "Good morning, little Bea. I'm your Aunt Tam."

Grandma slows to a stop in front of our new house, number sixty-three. I look up the dirt driveway, and along the bricks of the front walk, and at the heavy wooden door, and it's weird to think I'll be sleeping in this house next week. And so will Wendell and Cameron and Tucker and Bryce and Dodger and Roscoe and Fred. And it's weird to think that Aunt Tam will be two streets away instead of just on the other side of my bedroom wall.

Grandma nods toward the house across the road. "You know your neighbors?" I shake my head. Their garage is

14

full of boxes and a mattress leans against a car in the driveway, but what I'm really looking at is one of those practice nets in the yard that's regulation goal-sized and sends the ball bouncing back to you. Before Grandma starts driving slowly again, the front door swings open and a girl I've never seen before comes bounding out with a soccer ball beneath her arm. She's wearing stretchy jean leggings and a button-down blousy shirt and her brown, wavy hair is long and loose over her shoulders, and she's barefoot. I'm thinking she can't possibly have any kind of good touch on the ball dressed like that.

Then she drops the ball on the lawn and starts striking it against the net and dead trapping its return every time before striking again. Hard. With her left foot.

I'm wondering if she's in sixth grade too and if she can do a flip throw-in and if she was the Most Valuable Girl wherever she came from.

"Looks like there's another soccer star moving to Evergreen Road," Grandma says. "Should we say hi? Feels like a good day to make a new friend."

"Nah," I say. "We better go save Grandma Ethel."

Mom always says it's important to find friends who'll walk with you through the cold night, even if you're walking in circles. But I'm not made of whispery, walky, hot chocolate hugs. I think I'm more like the icicles that hang from the eaves, strong and sharp and fine on my own.

I like Nelle and Fern from my rec team, but we're not the hang-outside-of-school kind of buddies. Plus, I do have one friend. And I don't need more than Maximilian.

The girl strikes the ball hard again and Grandma shrugs and we drive off, down Evergreen and onto Maple. The Valentine house is a five-minute drive from our condo and I don't know why Mom and Wendell think that's not close enough. When we get there, Cameron is taping boxes together in the driveway and Tucker is practicing his piano, which has been moved out to the garage already.

They wave and smile and walk toward us when we drive up. Grandma Bea pulls them into a hug. "We were just missing you and wanted to say hi."

Cameron kind of screws up his face like *really?* and so do I because we saw them yesterday, but Tucker smiles and gets all misty and I swear he's going to snort like Wendell. Then Grandma pulls me into the hug and I'm all squished in with them until she says, "OK, that feels better. Your brother inside?" They nod.

On the way to the house Grandma leans in for an Embers-girls whisper, "I do love those boys, but you can't tell a couple of teenagers you're coming to check on them." I smile and Ethel creaks the door open like she really is a hundred years old.

"Oh, hello!" she says. "Come in, come in."

I'm about to say we are just checking to make sure everyone is alive and we'll be on our way back to the condo now, but Grandma says OK and before I know it Ethel is inching through all the moving boxes and making tea and offering me a rice cake. I shake my head because rice cakes are dry and tasteless and only one-hundred-year-olds, and Wendell, like them.

I see the little blue porcelain container on their kitchen windowsill and I wonder where Wendell will keep that in our new house and I'm hoping not on our kitchen windowsill because that would feel a little weird and sad. I want to stop thinking about those rings inside so I start looking for Bryce and I know right where I'll find him because Wendell said, clearly, twice, "No video games. If you want to hang out with your friends, hang out with them in real life."

I open the door to the basement and hear the sound of explosions. I'm right. I don't even have to go down to check so I say, "Grandma Bea, Bryce is playing video games."

"And we had M&M's for breakfast," she says, and gives me that same wink like this is our little secret.

And I'm thinking, of course. Bryce gets away with everything. Little things like extra screen time and big things too.

3

PRINCIPAL MEESLEY CALLED IT an innocent mistake. The truth is, Bryce deserved at least an in-school suspension on his record, but Meesley just thumped him on the shoulder and said, "Boys can be careless, but I think he learned his lesson. Am I right?" Bryce grinned and nodded.

I tried to tell Principal Meesley that Bryce wouldn't learn any lesson, but he waved me off and said that when I'm forty-three and looking back on Bryce Valentine spilling soap solution from science class down the hallway, I'll laugh. But I'll tell you one thing. Bryce didn't spill it. He poured it. And I won't laugh when I'm forty-three or ninety-nine or any other age. And I don't think Mr. Rinaldi and Ms. Long will either.

The soap that Bryce poured in the hallway was one of the solutions we were using to test tension, that thing that happens at the surface of liquids where all the little molecules hold on to each other so tightly that bugs can creep across without falling through. Little water bugs like Bryce Valentine who are held up by Meesley even when I'm trying to splash around and teach him what it feels like to fall in.

I'm pretty sure the soap in the hallway was meant for Maximilian because it was smeared right outside of Ms. Miller's science lab before lunch, and Maximilian is always the first one in and the first one out because he has to be two minutes early for everything. Plus, I saw Bryce and his two bonehead friends, Kenny and Morris, in the hallway, and they're always poking fun behind Maximilian's back. I was coming from the bathroom and they were taking long sips from the water fountain and watching Ms. Miller's door. They scurried away fast when it wasn't Maximilian's sneaker that found the slippery solution.

I told Principal Meesley that Bryce, Kenny, and Morris were the only three to leave the science lab that period, but when Meesley pulled them into the hallway they all clung together like little molecules, shaking their heads and saying it must have been an accident. That Bryce was carrying a measuring cup but he didn't mean to spill it.

I reminded Meesley that it's a rule that all science materials stay in the lab.

But Bryce got off with an apology letter to both limping teachers, who slid and surfed down the hallway, hands circling, until they slammed into each other and fell in a heap.

When I went home that day I told Mom everything and she said things like *I sure hope you're wrong* and *Wendell will talk to Bryce*. I told her I wasn't wrong, and that Bryce laughs along with Kenny and Morris when they make fun of Maximilian, and that Bryce will never get in trouble because Meesley is no better than a creeping water bug.

When I told Grandma she said, "Ah, they're still using the old *boys will be boys* hogwash." Then she put her arm around my shoulders and said, "You'll just have to show Bryce on the soccer field tomorrow."

And that's another reason why Grandma's a good captain. She reminds you there's more than one way to squash a water bug.

I'm a good captain too. Even if Wyatt Triggers was the actual captain of our rec team, everyone knows I ran that field. We won the rec soccer coed championship in fourth grade and we would have won again in fifth grade except we were playing against Bryce's team, the day after the soap-in-the-hallway incident, when he should have been suspended and not playing at all in the first place. The referee must have lost his whistle because Bryce was offsides by two yards and it cost us the game. Bryce knew it too because when his teammates started cheering and lifting him up on their shoulders he shot a glance at me like I-probably-*was*-offsides-but-the-referee-didn't-see-it *so ha.*

All the parents for our team were standing on the side where Bryce scored the game-winning goal and all the parents for their team were at the other end. Except for my mom and Wendell. They were standing together at the midline like they couldn't pick sides and were wishing we'd just tie in overtime.

But when Bryce received the last pass my mom jumped up and said, "Offsides, ref! Come on!" And for a minute I thought maybe she and Wendell would get in a fight and break up so they could each go to their own kid's side and we wouldn't ever have to have a wedding.

After the game Kenny and Morris waited until the ref and coaches turned their backs, then they laughed at our goalie, spit on the eighteen-yard line, and linked arms with Bryce as they walked off the field. And I'll tell you one thing. Kenny and Morris are the biggest, sneakiest bullies in the grade and Bryce is the biggest bully-follower-gets-away-with-everything-er there ever was.

After we huddled with our teams, and Kenny and Morris sauntered off, Bryce and I slung our bags over our shoulders and started walking to the sideline in the middle of the field where Mom and Wendell stood waiting.

"You were offsides," I said. "By a mile."

"Was not."

"Was too."

"Was not."

"Was too!" I say and shove my fingers in my ears so I can't hear his lying little voice.

Mom pulled me into a hug and said, "You played great, Bea. You can't win them all."

I looked at Bryce and was about to say *Actually I could win them all if everyone would play by the rules* but he was looking at the ground. He didn't even seem that happy that he won. He actually looked kind of sad. Like he didn't win at all. And that got me thinking about more than just the offside goal and losing the championship. It got me thinking of the day Bryce and I turned six weeks old, the day Wendell met my mom, and the rings in the blue porcelain container.

Then Bryce shook his head and sucked his teeth and

said, "I wasn't offsides. Even the ref—"

Wendell cut him off and said, "It looked close from here. But it's just a game." Wendell hates conflict.

Mom and Wendell quick-kissed goodbye and Bryce got in Wendell's car and they drove off like it was no big deal that he just stole the whole championship.

4

MOM AND WENDELL ARE home from their honeymoon, but now our condo is empty except for the two stools at the kitchen counter. Wendell has a set of four that he's bringing for the kitchen in the new house, and when we all eat together we'll sit at a new, long dining room table with space for a hundred seats and a high chair.

We're leaving our stools behind for the couple moving in so they can have nice, quiet dinners, just the two of them.

Everything we're taking is packed away under our carport and the stuff we're not bringing, including my bed, is at the end of our driveway. Mom's giving it to someone to sell at a yard sale and I'm getting Mom's big bed because she'll be sharing with Wendell now. That feels weird and I don't like thinking about it so I shake it out of my brain because it also means no more early morning stories in her room. I guess maybe I'm getting too big for those anyway.

Our front door opens and Maximilian walks in. He lives in the end unit with his grandparents and we stopped knocking on each other's doors as soon as we were big enough to reach the knob and turn.

"It looks weird in here," he says, looking around.

"Yeah, it does." I try not to think about all the important things that happened in this condo. I took my first step in the backyard, and decorated soccer ball birthday cupcakes with Mom at this counter, and ran the same route through the woods to the perfect climbing tree with Maximilian so many times that we stomped a path wide enough for us to run side by side. He taught me to read in that tree. And when we continued the path through to the other side of the woods, into the schoolyard playground, I taught him how to go across the monkey bars.

He shoves the glasses back up his nose. "I wanted to say bye, except it's not really bye, because I'll see you in school."

"Oh, Maximilian, you're welcome over anytime," my mom says. "You know that. And you don't have to knock on our new door either."

Except Maximilian and I know that's not true. It

won't be the same. Because Bryce doubles over and laughs when Kenny and Morris start breathing hard and pretend to spin out of control and yell *Help! I'm having a Max attack!* And who wants to walk through their own bully's door? Even if their only friend lives there too.

It's easy to not be nice to Maximilian. That's why some kids pick on him. His glasses are thick and slide down his nose a hundred times a minute and he likes things particular ways and if they don't go that way then he starts breathing hard and shaking his head no. And unless you really know him, you wouldn't know that he just needed a desk that's an even number away from the door but the teacher assigned him to the third one in, or that he needed to start walking with his left foot stepping first, but everyone got a little too close during lineup and he had to step with his right.

And not everyone knows that he has a spot between his thumb and pointer finger that you can squeeze and sometimes it helps him breathe normally again and stop shaking. And not everyone knows that when his mom comes to visit he runs away to our tree in the woods, and when she comes knocking at our door I never give up his hiding place, and I wait until she's driven off before I follow our stomped-down path and join him there.

"I'm pretty sure our walkie-talkies won't reach," he says.

I didn't even think of that, and now I'm feeling worse. "I'll try you tonight," I tell him. But I already know he's right.

My mom and his grandparents have a no-cell-phones-until-high-school rule so we saved up our allowances and got these cheap walkie-talkies at a yard sale when we were in fourth grade so we could talk past curfew. The signal was weak, but our condos were only twenty-eight steps apart. Maximilian counted.

Wendell pulls up to the curb in a long moving truck and toots the horn twice. He puts the truck in park, and hops down. Mom smiles at Maximilian and says, "Remember, anytime."

Then she walks out and Wendell hugs her in the front yard and I hear him say, "Happy day, Louise!"

I'm pretty sure he's about to start snorting but Mom says, "Don't you get all weepy on me right now, Mister. We have a truck to load." I can tell Wendell wants to make this a big moment, like saying *I do* and walking down the aisle as husband and wife, but Mom is clapping her hands like *chop chop.*

"Well, I guess I'll see you," Maximilian says. He puts his hands on the sides of my shoulders, which is his version of a hug.

"OK," I say.

Cameron pulls up in Wendell's car and parks in front

of the moving truck. Tucker hops out of the passenger seat and a basketball rolls after him. He dribbles it in our driveway a couple of times but then stuffs it back in the car. Tucker loves watching sports but he isn't very coordinated and he doesn't want to do anything that could even possibly injure his hands, because somehow he can make his fingers fly over the piano keys like it's nothing.

Bryce opens the back door and Dodger and Roscoe bound out and sniff around the mailbox. They both mark their territory, and it makes me mad because this is my territory. At least for another hour.

Maximilian leaves out the back and I go through the front door to the yard.

Wendell puts his hand on my mom's belly and tells her to sit on the old lawn chair at the end of the driveway and relax. "We have enough hands. And paws."

Too many, I'm thinking.

She starts to protest but Aunt Tam comes flying out the front door of her condo and says, "Don't you dare lift a finger, Embers!"

Mom huffs and sits and Wendell says, "Glad she'll listen to you."

Wendell, Cameron, Tucker, and Aunt Tam start loading the truck with our things. I drag my soccer net down the driveway, but it's not new, and the pieces are loose, so the crossbar keeps popping out from the posts.

28

I prop it up in the truck between a couch and a dresser.

Bryce is sitting on the grass trying to soothe Fred, who is screeching in his cat cage. "It's OK, Freddy Fred. We're almost home." Both dogs are circling Bryce and panting and rolling over for belly rubs. All the animals love Bryce the best and I have no idea why. I also have no idea how he called the new house *home* already. Home to me will always be this condo.

Mom points to me and then to Bryce and then to the bookshelf under the carport. I hesitate and she raises her eyebrows and mouths *go*. I sigh and shrug and try to move the bookshelf myself but it'll take me forever to wiggle-inch it down the driveway like this. Mom's watching me and pointing to Bryce like I should ask him for help but I'm not asking him for any help. I got this.

Then Wendell butts in and says, "Bryce, go give Bea a hand."

"I'll be right back, Freddy Fred," Bryce says and pats the cage. Then he jogs down the driveway and grabs a side. "One, two, three," he prompts, and we lift and hobble down the driveway sideways. But I don't need his help so I lift my side higher and move my feet faster and he whines *Quit it, Bea* and I say *Just keep up, Bryce* and we shuffle up the ramp into the truck and Wendell helps us lay it down. Then Bryce runs back to Fred.

This feels weird already. Our lamps and throw

pillows and bookshelves are all mixed up in the back of the truck with their couch and piano and kitchen stools and living room chairs.

When we're done loading, Tucker climbs into the back of the truck and sticks his hands under the piano cover and without even looking at the keys he plays a song about *goodbye, farewell* and something in another language. "From *The Sound of Music!*" he hollers and I know he's trying to be nice and funny, but I'm still just sad.

I hug Aunt Tam like we're moving to Alaska instead of Evergreen Road. "I'm going to miss sharing a wall with you," she tells me. "Even if the first year was all crying."

That makes my eyes burn, thinking about how Aunt Tam knew me from the very beginning, but I bite my tongue in the back of my mouth and tell her I'll visit a hundred times a week.

She hugs my mom too. "I'm happy for you," she says. "Now go blend."

Cameron gets in Wendell's car and Bryce lifts Fred's cage into the back with him. Dodger and Roscoe follow and curl up on the seat beside him. Tucker asks if he can drive but Cameron says *no* and Tucker says *oh come on* and Cameron says *just get in* and Tucker says *you stink* and Cameron says *you've had your license for like five minutes.*

Then finally Mom says, "Tucker, why don't you drive my car? I'd like to go in the truck anyway," and hands him her keys.

Tucker hollers, "Yes! Thanks, Louise!" and slams the door to our Toyota Camry and I'm thinking, *Really? We're sharing cars now too?*

Wendell, Mom, and I climb into the front bench seat of the moving truck, Wendell by the window, me in the middle, and Mom and the curve of her belly in the driver's seat. We pull away from the curb and away from the condo, and away from Aunt Tam and Maximilian and the stomped-down path to our climbing tree with Cameron and Tucker and Bryce and Dodger and Roscoe and Fred following behind us.

It takes us three minutes to get there but it feels like a hundred miles away from where I belong.

As Mom is backing the truck into our new driveway I check out the house across the road. The rebound soccer net is still set up and the garage doors are open. There aren't as many boxes in there now.

Cameron and Tucker park the cars on the road out front and Wendell helps Mom and me down from the truck and pulls us to the lawn. He waves the boys over and the dogs come bounding and Bryce carries Fred, still screeching in his cage. Then Wendell takes a deep breath and brings us all into a hug that feels sweaty and dog-panty, and I know Wendell wants some special blended family huddle but I just smush into my mom's shoulder and she sneaks me a little Embers-girls hip-check.

"I love you all so much," Wendell says, but before he can start snorting, the cat screeches again and ruins the moment. It's the first time I've ever liked that cat.

"Can we go inside now? Fred is freaking out." Bryce holds the cage in a hug.

Wendell takes Mom's hand and a dramatic breath like life will never be the same as soon as we walk in that door. And I'll tell you one thing, he's right.

"Ready?" he asks.

Mom links her arm in mine and says, "Come on."

I'm hoping the house will seem different than the last time I walked in with Mom and Wendell and the realtor. It was awkward then, like I was walking through a museum of another family's stuff.

When we toured through their house Mom kept telling me to imagine us living there. Imagine our stuff. "Can't you see us baking cookies in this kitchen?" she asked. I gave her a look that said we don't even bake cookies in our condo. Then she said, "Oh, fine. Can't you imagine us eating cereal in this kitchen?"

She was beaming and running her hand over the tiniest curve of her belly and so I just nodded and said, "Yeah, I could see that."

Wendell holds up the key and asks, "Who would like to do the honors?"

"You do it, Louise," Tucker says. My mom nods and turns the key and pushes open the door and we all step in and it doesn't feel like a museum anymore. It feels like an empty, echoey cave that smells like new paint.

Bryce rushes to the middle of the living room and opens Fred's cage. The squealing stops the second he pulls the cat out. "Sorry, Freddy Fred," he says. "But we're home now. No more cage." The cat rubs his head against Bryce's chest and starts purring.

Then the dogs burst in behind us, panting and wagging, and the boys run up the stairs to check out their bedrooms.

I feel Mom next to me. "What do you think?"

"A little empty," I answer.

She nods. "Agreed. But it'll fill up fast."

I'm pretty sure Mom's talking about filling it with furniture and memories and stuff, but I'm thinking about bodies. It'll fill up with Wendell and Cameron and Tucker and Bryce and Dodger and Roscoe and Fred and a new baby and it'll never be just the Embers girls anymore, at the counter, on two stools, with Corn Pops and elbow room.

Mom takes my hand. "Come on." We follow the boys up the stairs.

There are four small bedrooms and Mom promised I would have my own. Cameron and Tucker are sharing because Cameron will be a senior this year, and colleges are already offering him swim team scholarships, so they'll only be sharing for a year before he moves into a dorm room somewhere. He's the best butterflyer in New England and every once in a while when we drive to the lake he'll do a few strokes and fly across the roped-in area, his shoulders and arms lifting out of the water and stretching back under, and everyone stops and points and says, "Look at him go."

They decide they are going to split the room, literally, with a sheet down the middle. When Cameron graduates Tucker will take the sheet down and a year after that, Tucker will graduate too and probably go to some amazing school for music, then maybe the baby will move in.

Bryce has his own room. And so do I.

Mom and Wendell have a bathroom in their bedroom and the other bathroom has a shower and two sinks and Wendell keeps calling it the kids' bathroom like we're all part of the same family, like we're all just their kids now.

Cameron and Tucker are measuring the width of their room by counting toe-to-heel footsteps. "Twenty-four," Cameron says. Then he walks back twelve and stands in the middle and stretches out his long butterfly arms and says, "This is the imaginary line."

They start arguing about who gets the side with most of the window and Mom nudges me into the hallway and toward my room.

It's square and empty and smaller than Cameron and Tucker's, but it's bigger than my room in the condo, and it has a closet and a ceiling fan and a window that looks out over our sloping backyard.

"It'll feel like yours in no time," Mom says. She's walking around and pointing to where my bed could go and the bookshelf. But I cross my arms and say no, that my bed will have to go on the other side, away from that wall, because that's the wall I share with Bryce and I want to sleep as far away from him as I can. Mom takes a breath and runs her hand over her belly and I feel like a huge brat but I can't help it.

She rolls her eyes and says, "OK. How about your shelves, though? Can those touch this side? Or do you think it's too risky and your books might get contaminated?"

That makes me laugh a little even though I don't want to and Mom pulls me into a hug and says, "I love you, Bea." I can feel her bump between us.

Then I hear Tucker calling from downstairs. "Bea!"

I walk to the top of the stairs and look down at him.

"There's a new girl who lives across the road. She's in your class and she plays soccer! Come down!"

Mom's standing next to me now and giving me a look like *Bea, go.*

I walk down and out the front door and the girl is in her yard juggling a soccer ball in a blue dress and strappy sandals. She's taller than I am and has a serious shin guard tan below her knees and every time she steps I can see muscles flex in her legs.

"She can juggle longer than I can," Tucker says. I want to tell him that's not saying much at all.

I give a half wave to the girl. She waves back and doesn't miss a beat with juggling. I'm starting to think she might be able to juggle longer than I can too and I know I'm supposed to say something like *Whoa, nice skills*, but I don't want to because soccer's *my* thing and everyone in our town knows that. There are other girls who play, like Nelle and Fern and Cara from my grade in school, but they haven't been playing forever like I have. They only started in fourth grade. This girl looks like she might have been playing forever.

Then the girl dead traps the ball and calls, "I'm Aileyanna. People call me A."

"I'm Bea," I say.

She kind of laughs a little and taps the ball between her feet. "I'm going into sixth grade."

Then Tucker jumps in. "So is Bea! And so is my brother, Bryce. He's upstairs."

"He's not *my* brother, though," I tell her.

And I can see her face scrunch up like she's trying to figure out how the heck that all works because if you're not from our town already then we'll have to explain it.

"Well, I guess now he's your *step*brother," Tucker says.

I don't like that term, *step*. It sounds like they're a step-in, like a substitute for a player who never showed up or one who got tired and had to leave the game early, and here come Wendell and Cameron and Tucker and Bryce and Dodger and Roscoe and Fred to *step*-in. But we were fine, just Mom and me. A solid team.

"Their dad married my mom," I explain.

"Oh, cool," she says.

Then Tucker points to her soccer ball. "Bea plays too. She's really good."

She nods and says, "Awesome!" And tells me she's been playing on a travel team all summer and then goes on and on about how they scored in the last minute of their final game and it went past overtime and ended in a shoot-out and the whole time she's talking I'm thinking *Not fair.*

Then she flicks the ball up and balances it on her instep. "Where did *you* play this summer?"

I'm about to say *Just on my own down at the rec fields* and tell her that sometimes my Grandma Bea would come cheer me on or my aunt Tam would set up pine cones to dribble around and every once in a while I'd see some of the boys from school down there shooting on goal, but even in my head it sounds small. Like she really is some A-is-for-Aileyanna all-star, and I'm just Bea.

So I pretend I didn't hear her and say, "I should probably go help unpack." I gesture toward the house.

"Oh, OK." Then she flicks the ball up, strikes it hard against the rebound net, smooths out her dress, and I'm thinking, *Who dresses like that to play soccer?*

By dinner that night the moving truck is empty, and the garage is full of boxes. Wendell and Cameron return the truck while Tucker and Bryce move the furniture to where Mom points.

"One step to the left. Right there," she says and they lower the couch against the living room wall. Then they position Tucker's piano into the corner. The four stools from their house are pushed in to the kitchen counter and a rug that used to be in their TV room is rolled out across the floor. Mom disappears into the garage and comes back with our two throw pillows from the condo and tosses them in the corners of the couch.

They don't look right.

She helps me make my bed and push it to the not-Bryce side of my new room. We shake out her old comforter until the down is all light and feathery, lifting it above our heads and letting it settle slowly onto the sheets. It's the same blue comforter I'd snuggle under for a story when I'd wake up early in the condo and tiptoe into her room. She fluffs my pillows too and helps me center the bookshelf on the opposite wall, the share-Bryce wall, and we each lift a side of my desk until it's under the window.

I put my walkie-talkie on the windowsill and slide my boxes of clothes across the floor but I don't have any hangers yet, they're somewhere in the garage, so I just sit on the edge of my bed and Mom sits next to me.

"See? Feels better already."

I nod and she pats my hand with hers. Her finger has a new ring on it too, and unlike Wendell, she's never had one before. Never even wanted one. Only wanted me.

"I know," she says. "It'll take time."

Sitting with her here in my new room doesn't actually feel so bad. But it doesn't last more than a minute before we hear Wendell and Cameron get home and start carrying boxes from the garage into the bedrooms and bathrooms upstairs.

Then the doorbell rings and the sound isn't just a ding-dong chime like the condo, it's an eight note little jingly song that sounds like Christmas. My mom and I look at each other and make a face like we just took a bite of Corn Pops and the milk was sour.

"That's going to have to change," we say together and it makes us laugh a little while we stand up.

"Can someone please open the door before they ring that bell again?" Mom calls down the stairs.

"I kind of like it," Wendell says. "It's happy."

Mom gives him a look. "It's me or the bell, Wen."

He laughs and puts his hand on the knob.

"I don't get doorbells anyway," she says. "If you want something, you knock until you get an answer."

That's what she did when she was six months pregnant with me and fifty hours short of her training to becoming a paramedic. She'd been an EMT for five years pumping chests and giving breath and keeping bodies alive in the back of ambulances while they sped to the hospital in Burlington, and she wasn't about to give up her training for "desk work" until after I came. So she knocked hard on her supervisor's door. And before he could say anything she walked right past him, picked up the free weights in his office, and did sixty squats and thirty-five lifts and when she dropped the weights to his floor she said, "I think I can manage the work for

40

another fifty hours. I got this."

She wouldn't have met Wendell if she hadn't finished those fifty hours, if she hadn't become a paramedic, if she hadn't knocked on that door.

The guys who rang our jingly bell are here to deliver the new dining table and chairs. They turn it sideways, slide it through the door, and make a tight turn around the corner to where Mom is pointing. They unwind the bubble wrap from all the parts, screw on the legs, carry in the eight chairs, dust off the surfaces, and say, "That should do it."

Mom signs something and thanks the guys and before they've closed the front door, Wendell is running his hands over the edges and saying, "What are we waiting for? Let's try this out."

He takes his phone from his pocket to order dinner, and smiles at Mom when he says, "Actually, no, we've changed our address. Sixty-Three Evergreen Road."

He knows all of our orders by heart. I do too. We've had Chinese food enough together over the past two years since our first blended dinner. I was in fourth grade and I didn't want to go to Bryce Valentine's house, but Mom said, "Give it a try is all I ask." Bryce had been bragging in school about his two new chocolate Lab puppies so I said OK, but I made it clear I was going for the puppies.

The Chinese food came in three different bags and we didn't all fit at the Valentines' table so Bryce and I sat on the stools at their counter, which was only five steps away from the table, but felt like we were on a separate island. Dodger and Roscoe were squirmy and nippy but wouldn't leave Bryce's feet, even when we ate. Those became our seats every time we went to the Valentines' for dinner. Wendell, Mom, Cameron, and Tucker at the table, and Bryce and me at the counter arguing about whose elbow was crossing the invisible line between us, with Dodger and Roscoe at our feet.

The Valentines would come to the condo too sometimes and we'd all have pizza on the living room floor and watch the Olympics or the World Cup, which I didn't mind so much because Tucker knows a lot about sports and can't sit still when he's watching a close game.

Tonight is different. Because even though Wendell ordered the same three bags of Chinese food we've always ordered, tonight we're all sitting around the same table. And when we finish, no one is going home because we all live here now.

Mom sits at one head of the table and Wendell sits at the other. Cameron and I take up one side, facing Bryce and Tucker on the other. Dodger and Roscoe, who are definitely not puppies anymore, slide their thick bodies between Cameron and my chairs and curl up, one on each of Bryce's feet. Fred jumps on the windowsill behind Wendell and meows as we open the bags of take-out.

Mom and I share a little corner of the table and even though I'm expecting dinner to be weird, it isn't really. Maybe it's because I have my same order from Joyce's Chinese, number eighteen, shrimp lo mein, or maybe it's because even if the rest of the house is a mishmash of Valentine stuff with Embers stuff, this table is no one's, like we're playing on a neutral site.

It isn't until we have to take turns in the bathroom brushing our teeth, until it's time to get into pajamas, and when we start coming downstairs for cups of water and to search for a book or a phone charger, that it starts to feel weird. Every family has a time when no one else knows them. When you turn off the TV, take a shower, brush your teeth, unwind the rubber band from your hair, shimmy out of your pajama pants under the covers, and keep them stuffed in the bottom of your bed so they're warm for you in the morning. When you wake early and walk down the hall to your mom's room for a story beneath her comforter before breakfast.

It's weird to see Wendell and Cameron and Tucker and Bryce in those in-between times.

When Mom tucks me in tonight she closes the door and sits on the edge of my bed and kisses my forehead like she always does. She tells me she loves me all the way up to the Care Bears, which is our thing, and when she rubs the curve of her belly and gets up to leave I don't tap my goodnight knock-knock-knockity-knock on the wall to Aunt Tam and I keep my pajama pants on, because even under the comforter, and even with the door closed, it feels weird to take them off. Like if I have to pee in the middle of the night and I wander in the dark to the bathroom I might see Wendell or Cameron or Tucker or Bryce or trip over a dog and wake up the whole house and someone would turn on the light and then I'd be in my underwear.

I reach for the walkie-talkie and turn the dial on top. Static. "Bea to Maximilian. Over," I whisper. But it's just static and static and static.

When I close my eyes and try to sleep I have to bite my tongue in the back of my mouth and think *I got this.*

5

THERE'S SUN SHINING IN my face, and when I open my
eyes I don't know where I am. It takes lots of blinks to
adjust and remember.

New room. New house. New family.

I want to yell to Mom that we need blinds, thick ones
like in the condo. And I want to sneak down the hall
for a story in her bed before breakfast. But I just wait,
too hot in my pajama pants, and try to hear if anyone
else is up. It feels like my first sleepover party in third
grade when I zipped myself in a sleeping bag on Court-
ney Henderson's carpeted basement floor. I couldn't fall
asleep like everyone else did and I felt weird hearing all
their sleep sounds, like I shouldn't move an inch. So I
faked a stomachache and called my mom to come pick

me up and bring me back to my bed in the condo. I gave my knock-knock-knockity-knock on my bedroom wall to Aunt Tam, and in the morning, had a story with Mom under her comforter. I don't do sleepovers.

I can hear someone snoring now. It's probably Wendell. But it could be coming from Cameron and Tucker's room, or maybe it's a dog I'm hearing through the wall, curled up in Bryce's bed. And I don't feel like I should move an inch and I wish I could call my mom to come pick me up and bring me home.

I wait and listen as long as I can but I have to go to the bathroom so I tiptoe across my room and creak the door open. Then I walk fast down the hall and pull the bathroom door closed behind me.

When I finish, I rest my fingers on the flusher, but I don't know whether I should flush or not. I don't want to wake anyone up and then run into them in the hall because this is one of those in-between times. But I also don't want to have my pee and toilet paper floating around in the bowl either, just waiting for someone to lift the lid and go *ewwww*. I decide to flush. Then I turn the faucet on to a trickle, wash my hands, and when I turn it off, I hear footsteps pass by the door so I freeze. When it's silent again, I turn the knob, pull it open slowly, and tiptoe fast down the hall and back into my room, inch the door closed, then nearly scream when I jump into my bed and my mom is there, under my comforter.

"Mom!"

"Sorry," she whispers. "I didn't mean to scare you."

She holds open the comforter and I snuggle down like I used to at the condo, both our heads on the same pillow. Then she shows me three fingers.

I huff a sigh. "One," I say. "That I don't have to divide my room down the middle with a sheet."

Mom laughs. "That's a really good one. Definitely something to be grateful for."

"Two, Chinese food leftovers. And three . . . Fred isn't screeching in that cage anymore."

That makes Mom laugh again, then she says, "OK, my turn. One, this quiet moment right now before everyone wakes up. Two, that this baby doesn't have your soccer feet, at least not yet." She puts my hand on her belly and waits.

I feel the baby kick and pull my hand away. "Yeah, that kid's got nothing on my left foot," I say.

Mom smiles. "And three . . . Chinese food leftovers. I swear I could eat those right now."

We hide our laughs in the comforter. Then Mom starts, "Once upon a time . . ." And even if someone is snoring, and Bryce is on the other side of my wall instead of Aunt Tam, and there's a baby between Mom and me, and nothing else feels the same as the condo, at least right now I'm getting an early-morning-under-comforter story.

The story is about a squirrel with an umbrella who has to keep making room for other animals, a raccoon, a cow, a bear, and eventually they all have to climb a tree to cover a giraffe. My mom's stories are always about animals doing silly things and every time we end up laughing at how the animals never go together.

"Where would you ever find a raccoon, a cow, a bear, and a giraffe, Mom?"

"In my story," she answers. Then she kisses my forehead and says she has to start getting ready. "Ultrasound today."

She pushes up from my bed and walks toward the door. "Cameron's got his last day of lifeguarding and Tucker's giving piano lessons to the Benson kids this morning. Not sure what Bryce is up to." She puts her hand on the knob. "Why don't you come with me?"

"That's OK," I say.

I went to her first ultrasound appointment and all the doctor stuff made me kind of woozy. When the technician pointed out the baby's kidneys and the chambers of its heart I said I had to go to the bathroom and found the nearest bench in the hallway. I slumped down with my head between my knees and took deep breaths until I felt normal. And when I walked back in the technician was asking my mom, "Are you sure you don't want to know what you're having?"

Mom wiped the goop from her belly and pulled her shirt back down. "I know what I'm having," she said. "A baby."

I don't want to get all hospital-woozy again so I tell her, "I think I'll look for the hangers in the garage and unpack some stuff here."

"OK." She kisses the top of my head and disappears down the hall.

When I get downstairs Cameron is scrambling eggs, and Bryce is looking for the toaster to cook his Pop-Tart. Tucker's already taken Wendell's car to the piano lesson, and both the dogs are wagging their tails with leashes hanging from their mouths.

"Forget it," Bryce says and tears open the Pop-Tart package. "I'll eat it cold." He clips Dodger and Roscoe into their leashes with his other hand and they all three wiggle out the door to the garage together. "We'll be back!"

Wendell comes in wearing sweatpants and a T-shirt and I can tell from his hair which side he slept on. I have eggs with Wendell and Cameron and then Mom comes down and finishes what's left in the pan.

Cameron dumps his plate in the sink and says, "Gotta go."

"Me too," says Mom.

Wendell swallows his last bite. "Tucker has my car."

Mom and Cameron kind of look at each other for a second. "I can drop you on my way if we hurry," Mom says.

"But I . . ." Cameron starts.

"Go," Wendell says.

"But Dad, it's the last day, and no one else gets dropped off to their job by their parent."

I want to say that's fine then because my mom isn't his parent.

"OK, Cameron," Wendell says. "Louise will just miss the ultrasound appointment to check on the health of your little sibling so you can drive yourself to lifeguarding and let the car sit in the lot all day."

Cameron rolls his eyes and grabs his swim bag from the counter. "Fine. Let's go."

"Thanks, Louise," Wendell says. "You sure you don't want me to come?"

"I'm sure I want you to have ten more boxes unpacked before I get home."

Mom squeezes my shoulders then grabs the keys and heads out behind Cameron.

"I'll be going through boxes in the basement first," Wendell tells me and sets his plate on the counter because the sink is full. "And don't worry about the dishes. I'll load and run the dishwasher as soon as I find the box with the detergents."

I nod but really I'm thinking we never used the dishwasher in our condo because we never had enough dishes to put in there and how can a sink be overflowing when it's only eight thirty in the morning and one kid only had a Pop-Tart?

Wendell heads downstairs and just like that, I'm alone.

Fred meows and slinks around the corner to remind me that actually, I'm not. But close enough, I'm thinking, and for some reason it feels just as weird to be alone in this house than it did two minutes ago with everybody shuffling, cooking, eating, wagging, complaining, and leaving.

I find a box of hangers in the garage and bring them upstairs. The tape peels off easily and as I'm hanging shirts in my closet and folding pants for the shelves, I'm thinking about starting school tomorrow, and what I should wear. Probably the same thing I'm wearing now. Overalls. I have two pairs of Carhartt overalls that are soft and broken in and when it's warm I roll them up and wear them with a T-shirt and flip-flops, and when it's cold I roll them down and wear them with a sweatshirt and boots.

I'm not usually nervous for the first day, but tomorrow

is middle school. It's the same building, but a different wing, with different teachers, and an actual middle school soccer team that plays against other schools. Well, a boys' soccer team anyway, which isn't fair, but our school is small and there's never been enough girls who want to play to field a whole team. Principal Meesley is the coach, and he lets the girls play for the boys' team if they want, but even if a few start the season, they end up on the bench for most of the games, then get bored and quit.

I'm not going to quit.

I fold a pair of overalls and a T-shirt and leave them out for tomorrow. Then I hear the sound of a well-struck soccer ball and the squeak of the rebound net and even though I don't want to go into Bryce's room and see all his slept-on pillows and clothes all over the place, I dash in quick to look out his window and across the street.

She's wearing a skirt and a fleece jacket and a pair of bright green Diadora cleats. The cleats look new. I want to throw open the window and call out *Why are you kicking a ball in a skirt?* But I just watch her take one more left-footed strike then go back to my room.

I'm cleaning out my backpack and putting my new notebooks in so I can have a fresh start for sixth grade and looking for that zip pouch where I keep all my pencils and erasers and I'm trying to ignore that sound of

Aileyanna shooting the soccer ball over and over. But every time I hear it, I bite down harder on my tongue and I picture her showing up for the boys' team and winning Most Valuable Girl and even though I think a trophy like that belongs in the trash, I don't want someone else to get it. She strikes the ball hard again and I drop my notebooks back in the box and hustle downstairs to the garage.

She's not the only girl with a strong left foot.

I find my yard sale soccer goal in the back corner of the garage. It's in three pieces and the net is all tangled and there are too many boxes in the garage to lay it out and set it up so I drag it to the yard.

Aileyanna traps the ball.

I can feel her watching me as I slide the plastic crossbar pieces into the goalposts and work my fingers to unknot a section of the net.

"Need help?" she calls.

I don't look up. "I got this."

She kicks the ball again.

I have the goal up, but the net is saggy and I'm thinking of finding a couple of sticks to use as stakes, but I forget that, and lace up my Diadora cleats. Mine are used and they're just black. I don't need a flashy color for people to notice my footwork. I find my ball in a box in the garage and juggle it a few times on my thighs then down to my feet and strike it, out of the air, with the instep of my left foot, into the upper right-hand corner of the goal.

The net isn't laced into the bars tightly enough so the ball escapes through the back and rolls under the evergreen trees.

Aileyanna strikes hers and it bounces back to her foot.

We go like that for at least ten more shots, back and forth, without saying anything, and without missing. Me, running for my ball and pulling it out from under the pine needles after each goal. Her, chest-trapping and juggling and taking it out of the air. And I know we're both waiting to see who'll be the first one to shank it.

Then Aileyanna's mom opens the front door and says, "A, your father's calling. Do you want to talk to him?"

She dead traps the ball and looks quick across the road. Our eyes meet and I'm trying to give her a look that says *I could do this all day and never miss. Might as well quit now.*

"Fine," she says and takes the ringing cell phone from her mom. Then she juggles the ball back into the garage and disappears.

I sit down on our front step, rolling the ball beneath my feet, and from this angle I can see right into

Aileyanna's garage. She's sitting on a box, looking down at her cleats. The phone is next to her.

I'm wondering if she's going to come out for more goals. I want her to know that just because she's A and I'm Bea and she has a summer travel team and my net is falling apart and my cleats are handed down doesn't mean I can't match her goal for goal.

When Mom gets home, ten boxes are unpacked, broken down, and stacked in the garage to be recycled. Wendell's T-shirt is sweaty but he gives Mom a hug anyway.

"The goal looks great, Bea!"

I want to tell her not really, that the net sags and the ball escapes through the back, but I begged her for it at the yard sale, and it's better than nothing.

Then Aunt Tam drives up and parks her car on the road. "Embers! Pictures!" she calls and joins us on the front step.

Mom pulls out a strip of ultrasound pictures and says, "There's your little sibling, Bea." She traces her fingers down the curve of the baby's back and along its curled-up legs, telling me what each picture is, but the only one I can really make out is the profile of the face. Forehead, nose, chin.

"The baby has your nose," Aunt Tam tells me.

"Identical," Mom agrees.

I smile because I guess that's good, and because I kind of see it. Our noses.

"Let's hope it doesn't have your epic, all-night cries," Aunt Tam adds, and throws her arm around me. I laugh and scooch closer to her and Mom scooches in too so we all three look like a defensive wall set up for a free kick, and Wendell's standing there in front of us looking at the strip of pictures with watery eyes and getting all snorty and blocking our sun. And I feel terrible for even thinking it, but I wish he weren't here. I wish that this baby was just Mom's and Aunt Tam's and Grandma Bea's and mine. Not his too. And not Cameron's and Tucker's and Bryce's and all the darn pets'.

Mom pats my knee and asks if I've seen that new girl across the road today, but just then Tucker gets home from the Benson kids' piano lesson and Bryce and the dogs come bursting out of the house. Tucker is asking Wendell if he can use the car to go see a friend and Wendell is saying, "We have so much to do here and Louise and I are both back to work tomorrow." And Mom is muttering that maybe they didn't take enough time off for the move and Tucker is whining that it's the last day before school starts.

After a few more back-and-forths Wendell says OK and Tucker takes off. Then Bryce starts screwing the garden hose to the spigot to fill water bowls for Dodger and Roscoe.

And I'm kind of glad for all the commotion because Mom forgets she asked about Aileyanna. I don't really want to talk about her, even though I'm still watching her just sitting on the box in the back of her garage, rolling the soccer ball between her green cleats.

Wendell hands the pictures back to Mom and she puts them on the front step so she can help Bryce with the hose, and Aunt Tam is pulling me into a big hug and saying how much she loves me and she'll see me soon, and Wendell is back in the garage breaking down more boxes, and just like that, I'm on the stoop, alone again.

Then I look down at the ultrasound pictures and find that swoop of the baby's nose. And I'll tell you one thing. This baby is an Embers all right.

6

THERE'S A QUIET KNOCK on my door. "Morning, Bea," Mom whispers.

She sits on the edge of my bed, dressed in her short-sleeved paramedic uniform. It has stretchy sides and extra space for the baby because during her last shift before the wedding she picked up the next-sized uniform but it was still tight across her belly and baggy everywhere else. So she knocked on her supervisor's door and said she needed a maternity medium before she popped out of these buttons while administering CPR.

"Three," she whispers to me.

I sigh and clear my throat and think of three things I'm grateful for. "One, that Maximilian's still in my class. Two, new teachers. And, three . . . real soccer league. Even if it's a boys' team."

Mom smiles and says, "Good ones. Now get up, sixth grader."

So I throw back the comforter, but this is not how the first morning of school is supposed to go. It's supposed to be a quick shower, a bowl of Corn Pops, and out the door with Maximilian down the tramped-down path to school.

Not this year. This year it's a line for the shower, and somehow I'm second to last. It's gloppy oatmeal that's been sitting in the pot, brushing my teeth in a sink next to Bryce Valentine, and having wet, out-of-shower hair in front of people other than my mom.

"Your hair is down," Bryce says.

"You're brilliant," I reply.

"It looks weird."

"You look weird."

Mom says to cut it out and kisses the top of my head. "I'll see you tomorrow morning," she says. "Have a great first day!"

She works a twenty-four-hour shift, then has two days off, then works another twenty-four hours. I used to like that schedule because it meant she was home a lot and when she wasn't, Grandma Bea would sleep over, and Aunt Tam would check in on me. But now I'll just be here with Wendell and Cameron and Tucker and Bryce and Dodger and Roscoe and Fred.

Wendell's wearing his hardware polo shirt with his name stitched on it and a pair of jeans with paint smudged on them, which is the unofficial uniform at the hardware store he manages in town. He hugs Mom and says, "Be safe. Drive slowly."

Mom slugs him in the arm and says, "Kind of defeats the point of an ambulance." They put their mugs in the sink and Mom grabs her overnight duffel and they both head out to the driveway. Their car doors slam at the same time and they start their engines and drive off down Evergreen Road.

My hair is hard to put up when it's wet, but the bus comes in six minutes and I never wear it down at school, so I make a messy blob with the rubber band around my wrist. Then we all grab our backpacks and head out. Cameron and Tucker turn left for the bus stop that goes to the high school, and I walk three steps behind Bryce toward the bus stop to our school.

When we get to the end of the road, Bryce gives Morris a high five and Aileyanna is already there too, waiting with her mom, who is taking a hundred pictures.

Aileyanna's wearing jeans that are skinny to her legs with brown boots that stop at her ankle. But not real boots, like winter boots or mud season boots. Her boots are soft-looking, and have a zipper down the side, and little wooden heels that make her even taller and they look like they would wilt in a one-inch puddle. Her hair is wet, and down, long over her shoulders. We look at each other and kind of half smile and for one second I think she probably won't even sign up for soccer when she finds out it's a boys' team.

Then I hear Morris say, "So wait, are you and Bea officially twins now?"

Bryce tells him to shut up, but he doesn't say it harsh enough, like Morris *better* shut up *or else.*

"Isn't that what a brother and sister with the same birthday are called?" he continues, laughing.

Bryce is just standing there like a dummy because he'll never really say anything to Morris, but there's a fire burning hot in my belly and my hands reach out and yank Morris in by the straps of his new backpack. His face is six inches from my face, which is good because I have a lesson he needs to hear loud and clear.

"He's not my brother."

I push him away before Aileyanna's mom gets to me. "Excuse me," she says, then goes on about how *we don't use our hands, blah blah blah.* I keep my mouth shut, but really I want to tell her I already have a mom, and a whole bunch of other people and animals pretending to be my family, so if she wants to butt in, she can tell Morris to shut his mouth.

Morris shakes his backpack back in place and mumbles something about how maybe I'm actually the brother and Bryce must be the sister. Bryce laughs him off like it's no big deal but I shoot him a look as the bus pulls up.

Aileyanna gives her mom a hug and gets on first and sits in the front. I'm next and I sit in the middle by myself, then Morris and Bryce go to the last seat in the back and Morris tells the kids sitting there to move and they do and then he tells Bryce to push in to the window.

I'm thinking about Maximilian walking down our path by himself right now and it makes me mad that I have to start my day telling Morris to keep his mouth shut and listening to the new girl's mom and riding on this stinky bus.

The teachers are waiting outside the school by the bus line holding posters to lead us into our new classrooms. I look for the sign that says *Ms. Blaise and Ms. Kravitz* and I push through the crowd and go stand next to Maximilian. I let my shoulder just barely touch his to let him know I'm there.

"Hey," he says.

"Hey."

"The walkie-talkies don't work."

I nod. "I know."

Ms. Blaise starts counting down the line. I follow her finger. A seventh grader named Tess who was on my rec team two years ago is in our class. I heard she quit the school team last year because she didn't want to play with the boys. Fern is in our class too, but not Nelle. Then Ms. Blaise's finger counts Kenny and Morris and Bryce. And even though I was 99 percent sure they would all be in my class again, it sinks in deep, right into that fire in my belly, when I see them there at the back of the line.

At the end of last year Mom and Wendell called the school and tried to get Bryce and me in different classes for sixth grade. It's school policy to separate siblings when they can, which actually happens a lot since there are only three middle school classes and they're multi-age, sixth through eighth grade. And even though Bryce Valentine and I are *not* siblings, I hoped the school would split us up anyway. But we're both supposed to be in a special class that has two teachers and there's only one of those so we're stuck together. Just like we have been since second grade.

Kenny and Morris get the special two-teacher class too.

Then I see Aileyanna walking up to the front like she's never seen a line before. She tells the teachers her name and says she wants to double-check that she's in the right place. Ms. Blaise looks down at her clipboard and says, "Aileyanna Absalon. Yes, right here. Top of the list." I roll my eyes.

Aileyanna doesn't go back to the end of the line, she stays at the front on the other side of Maximilian until Ms. Blaise says, "OK, all here!"

And Ms. Kravitz says, "Follow us!"

Our classroom doesn't have any desks. It has tables and benches and a big rug area with its own corner library and a couch and two big chairs like the ones we used to have in the condo and little fold-up camping chairs stacked on the shelf next to bins and bins of books. Ms. Blaise tells us that this will be our homeroom and our English class and that we can find a seat at one of the tables.

Maximilian and I take a table near the front and Kenny rushes to the couch.

"At a table," Ms. Blaise repeats.

Kenny sighs and tosses his backpack on a seat toward the back. Morris and Bryce join him.

Aileyanna sits at the table next to Maximilian and me, and Laurel and Georgia, who are both eighth graders, immediately join her and start asking where she got her boots and where she's from and Aileyanna switches her hair from one shoulder to the other and says, "Brooklyn."

Laurel and Georgia just kind of stare at her. "You're from New York City? Why'd you move?"

I'm wondering the same thing.

"My mom can do her job over the computer and she wanted a quieter, slower life," she says. "So here we are."

I want to say *a quieter, slower life? What's that supposed to mean?* but Ms. Blaise is calling for our attention and telling us to take out a notebook and something to write with, which makes a couple of kids groan but I'm good with that because I'm not one for first-day icebreaker games.

"My name is Ms. Blaise." She writes her name at the top of her own notebook and projects it on the SMART Board.

Then she reads us a story about a girl named Esperanza whose name means *hope*, and even though I don't understand it all, I like the way it sounds.

Now it's our turn, she tells us, to write everything we know about our own names. "You can make a list, write a poem, draw a picture, tell us what you know about it, what you don't know about it, if you like it, or don't." Then she starts a timer and says, "Four minutes."

Ms. Kravitz is helping the table behind us get started. She whispers a few words but then it's quiet. Maximilian taps the eraser of his pencil four times against the table before he starts writing.

Bea Embers, I start. Then I keep going.

And when the time is up I actually kind of like what I wrote. It doesn't sound as music-y and poem-ish as that

Esperanza story Ms. Blaise read to us, but it felt easy to write and it takes up almost a quarter of a page, which is the most I've ever written in the first four minutes of a school year ever.

We share at our tables and I tell Maximilian about being named after my grandma Bea, which is OK by me because Grandma Bea is strong, and funny, and puts M&M's in pancakes. Maximilian already knows all this, and I know that his mom gave him the name Maximilian and that it means *greatest*, and that even if she got everything else wrong, at least she got that right, because Maximilian *is* the greatest.

Then Ms. Blaise tells us we're all going to share something from our work. Some kids groan again. "It can be just one word," she tells us. "Or one line, or the whole thing. Whatever you feel comfortable telling us."

Hands shoot in the air. Not mine.

Ms. Kravitz calls on Aileyanna first. And Aileyanna doesn't just read a line from her seat. She stands up and reads the whole darn thing.

"I'm Aileyanna Absalon. People call me A." I look down at my paper and roll my eyes. Then she starts reading to us about her two grandmas, Ailey and Anna, and how her parents named her after both of them.

I bite my tongue in the back of my mouth because

I want to shout that she copied me except of course she had to go showing off with two grandmas and a hundred syllables. But I'll tell you one thing. I wouldn't want a fancy name like Aileyanna anyway.

She's reading from her page about how Absalon was an important name way back from some lords in Britain or something. Ms. Blaise is nodding her head and when Aileyanna finishes she claps her hands and says, "Thank you for sharing, A."

Laurel and Georgia say, "Good job, A," and just like that, everyone is calling her A. But I'll tell you another thing. I'm not.

Fern stands up next and says in a quiet voice that she'll just share one line. "My name is from *Charlotte's Web*," she says. "My mom's favorite book." I nod at her like *That's cool* because I didn't know that.

Kenny scoffs and says under his breath, "You were named after a pig?" and Morris starts laughing and snorting like a pig. I whip around and see Bryce hiding little laughs behind his hand.

Then Ms. Kravitz stands up and says, "Oh, you got that quite wrong, young man. You can make it your homework tonight to find out the pig's name in *Charlotte's Web*."

Kenny smirks and mumbles, "Whatever."

"Not whatever," Ms. Kravitz says. "It's her name." Then she turns to Fern. "Thank you for sharing, Fern. I love that book too."

Morris and Bryce are still muffling little laughs and Ms. Blaise says, "And you two. You can make that your homework as well since you think it's so funny."

And if I were more of a hugger, I'd want to hug her. And Ms. Kravitz too. Because for the first time in a hundred years Kenny and Morris and Bryce Valentine aren't getting away with something.

"And you can go next, please," Ms. Kravitz says, pointing to Kenny. He doesn't stand, but he mutters, "My dad gave me his name. That's why I'm Kenny. Kenny Junior."

"Thank you for sharing, Kenny," Ms. Kravitz says, and she says it like she really means it, like Kenny Junior just told her something really important. Kenny nods.

When it's Maximilian's turn he taps his pencil eraser four times on the table, stands up, and says. "Maximilian. Not Max."

Kenny and Morris and Bryce don't laugh out loud, but I can feel them smirking. I can feel it all the way from the back of the room and through my Carhartt overalls and straight into the fire in my belly.

I want to tell them they better keep their mouths

shut and that Maximilian likes to be called Maximilian because it's an even ten letters, unlike Max. But I think that will make them want to smirk and laugh harder so I just whisper, "Good job."

Then it's my turn to share but when I look down at my paper I don't know which part to read. "Bea Embers," I say. Then I skip the whole part about Grandma Bea, which feels bad, but who wants to hear about one grandma when they just heard a whole page about two grandmas? So I read the last part. "Embers. Like a fire. Ready to spark."

Ms. Blaise nods and says "wonderful" and thanks me for sharing.

A seventh grader shares that her dad just liked the way Quinn sounded, then Georgia says her mom let her older sister pick her name. She shrugs and says, "It could have been a lot worse. She was obsessed with *My Little Pony*. I could be Little Pony Ludlow." That makes everyone laugh.

Mac is named after his grandpa, who works at the hardware store with Wendell, and Wyatt says his mom has a thing about *W*'s. His brother is Warren and his sister is Winnie. Maddie's real name is Madeline, which is also her mom's name.

When it's Bryce's turn he looks down at his paper and says in the smallest voice I've ever heard him use,

"Bryce was my mom's maiden name."

Ms. Blaise thanks him for sharing and I turn around kind of slowly so he doesn't notice and I look at him because I didn't know that about his name and I didn't know that Bryce could have a small voice and that he could talk about his mom on the first day in a new class.

After everyone shares, Ms. Kravitz says, "We'll certainly remember your names now."

Then our classroom door flies open and Principal Meesley walks in. He didn't even knock.

"Sorry for the interruption," he announces. "In addition to being your principal, I am also the boys' soccer coach. I'm posting the sign-ups in the hallway. Write your name by end of day if you want to play." He holds up a list. Then he leaves.

Ms. Blaise waits for the door to close and says, "What he meant to say was *Welcome back! We're so excited for another year with you.*" Everyone laughs and Aileyanna leans over and whispers, "Who's the girls' coach?"

The bell rings. I shrug and tell her we just have a boys' team because not enough girls play. "We're allowed to sign up if we want," I say. I look down at her skinny jeans and flimsy fashiony boots and add, "You probably don't want to, though. All the girls end up quitting anyway." I don't tell her that *I'm* going to be the first girl that sticks. Not her.

She scrunches up her eyebrows. "No girls' team?"

Ms. Kravitz quickly hands out our schedules and walks us down the hallway to our next class. She comes to every class with us. That's part of the special two-teacher class thing.

Aileyanna is at the front of the line but she peels off when we pass the soccer sign-up sheet and writes *A* on the list. I peel off too and write *Bea* on the next line.

Later, when we pass by the list on our way to the lunchroom, I can see that the sign-up is so full of names already that kids had to start writing in more numbers all the way down to twenty-three. I put my finger right on the page to count the girls. A, Bea . . . Fern, Nelle, Cara . . . Jamie, Quinn. Seven That's more girls than ever before.

At lunch I sit next to Maximilian. Across from us, Tess is unwrapping a sandwich. "Hey, is it true you quit soccer last year?" I ask her.

She nods and says it was no fun on the boys' team. "Principal Meesley basically ignores the girls and so then the boys do too. They never pass."

I tell her there are seven girls already signed up this year and I'm thinking it might be harder to ignore seven. She looks down at her sandwich and says, "I babysit sometimes after school now." I shrug and say OK, but really I'm thinking that sounds awful.

We're not supposed to leave our class table during lunch, but Nelle sneaks over and squeezes in next to Fern and she waves to me too. "Did you have a good summer?" she asks.

I think about the wedding and Wendell and Cameron and Tucker and Bryce and Dodger and Roscoe and Fred and the moving van and leaving the condos and Maximilian and having to take the bus, but I just say, "Yeah. It was OK."

My milk carton is sticking and I have to poke my finger in to open the drinking spout, which is gross and annoying and I'm hoping no one is paying attention.

When I look up Nelle is smiling at me and I don't want her to say anything about the carton so I ask, "Did you see how many girls are on the soccer list?"

Georgia hears me and looks up. "How many?"

I hold up seven fingers and Mac, who was watching us from the end of the table, nearly spurts his milk. "Seven?" he says. "We're going to have to get another bench."

Kenny laughs. "No, they'll quit."

Tess rolls her eyes and Georgia tells them to shut their mouths and that they know nothing. They listen because she's in eighth grade but I can tell they're still snickering.

"I have to tell Emmie," Georgia says. Then she scans

72

the lunchroom, checking out where the aides are, and when they're not looking she sneaks off to another class table.

At the end of the day, on our way back to Ms. Blaise's room, I check out the soccer list again. It's so full of names now that it's down to the bottom and it makes me stop completely, right in the middle of the hall, and Maximilian slams into me.

"Bea!" he says.

And I tell him I'm sorry because I'm pretty sure I messed up his stepping and he had to do two left steps in a row. He's breathing hard like he's trying to catch his breath and Morris is laughing and saying, "Everyone take cover, Max is about to blow!" And I want to slug him for calling Maximilian *Max* because he just shared about that this morning and it makes everything worse and I have to sneak a between-the-thumb-and-forefinger squeeze.

Then Ms. Kravitz is there and she's counting by eights and I don't know why but it's working because Maximilian is with her by sixty-four.

But I'm doing my own counting. I'm counting down the girls on the list. A, Bea . . . Fern, Nelle, Cara . . . Jamie, Quinn . . . Georgia, Emmie, Micah . . . Tess. Eleven. A whole team.

* * *

After dismissal I carry the sign-up list to Principal Meesley's office. It says *Do Not Disturb* on the door. I give it a good knock.

"Busy," he calls through the door.

Aileyanna's behind me even though I didn't invite her to tag along, because she still can't believe we've never had a girls' team before. "Guess we'll try tomorrow," she says.

Maybe that's what an Absalon would do. Just try again later. But I'm an Embers. An Embers knocks again.

"Busy," he calls louder, and his secretary, Ms. Landry, asks if she can help me with something.

"I got this," I tell her, and knock again.

I hear his rolly chair slide toward the door. Then it opens. When he sees us outside, he stands up and says, "I said . . ."

But I shove the list toward him. "Eleven girls."

He takes the list, looks it over, folds it, and says, "You're going to miss your bus."

I have a hundred things I want to say to him like *That's it?* And, *Eleven's a whole team!* And, *Who's our coach?* And, *When's our first practice?*

But before I can say anything he takes a step forward, which makes us stumble two steps back and out of his office, and then his door is shut and we're on the other side and he's calling out, "Andrea, office is closed!"

Ms. Landry kind of smiles at us like *sorry* and I kind of smile back at her like *sorry*. Sorry your desk has to be so close to Meesley and you have to listen to him all day.

"Try again tomorrow," Ms. Landry says, and gives us a nod.

On the way to the bus I'm telling Fern and Tess and Georgia how Principal Meesley didn't say anything about our eleven-girl team, and how he just folded the list like he didn't even care.

"He's totally going to make us play with the boys again," Tess says. She tucks her thumbs under the straps of her backpack as we walk outside. "If he does, I quit. Back to babysitting."

"Same," says Georgia. "And I know Emmie will too."

And that gets my heart beating fast because I don't want anyone thinking about quitting yet. Tess sees her dad's car and says she has to go. She runs off, and Georgia and Fern get on their bus and say they'll see us tomorrow.

Our bus is the second in line and as we walk toward it I'm trying to ignore the clicking of Aileyanna's heels on those good-for-no-season boots.

"What position do you play?" she asks.

"Center midfield," I tell her.

She stops, fast, and puts her hands on her hips and

looks me right in the eyes and says, "That's my position."

"Number ten," we both say at the same time.

And I'll tell you one thing. She might have been center midfield and number ten in Brooklyn but that's my position here and there's no way I'm giving it up to some two-grandma'ed-summer-travel-league-people-call-me-A-Aileyanna.

7

MOM CALLS FROM THE hospital after dinner to ask how
the first day went and when I tell her about eleven girls
signing up for soccer she cheers so loud I have to hold the
phone away from my ear.

Bryce is scooping Fred's raw-fish-vomit-slop cat food
out of the can and I'm not even saying anything about
how disgusting it is because I'm still thinking about how
he has his mom's maiden name, but then he rolls his
eyes when he hears my mom cheering "Go, girls, go!"
through the phone.

I tell her I'll see her tomorrow and when I hang up I
say, "What? You think a girls' team is funny?"

Bryce shrugs his shoulders like *maybe* and I know
he's only rolling and shrugging and acting all cool

because Kenny and Morris were laughing about it at school, because Kenny and Morris have three brain cells combined.

"You're just mad because the boys' team will stink worse than Fred's dinner now that I won't be on it."

"Ha!" he says, "You'd be sitting the bench if you were on the boys' team, and you know it."

"If I *sat* the bench, you wouldn't even have a *spot* on the bench, you'd be in the grass at my feet."

Wendell comes downstairs and says, "Hey, hey. Come on. Quit it."

But Bryce can't quit it so he whispers, "MVP," like he even deserved that award last year.

And I'll tell you one thing. I'm glad there are ten other girls interested in soccer this year so I don't have to pretend to be teammates with Bryce Valentine.

"The girls' team is going to be great," Wendell says. "And for the record, I think Bea is an MVP too."

"MV*G* maybe," Bryce says.

I'm about to make him eat Fred's cat food when Wendell says, "Bryce, you know Bea is a force. Quit it."

Bryce grabs Fred and says, "Whatever. You're just saying that because you like Louise so you have to pretend to like Bea." Then he walks upstairs and slams his door.

Wendell takes a step toward the stairs but then

stops and looks back at me. Right when I think he's going to go up after Bryce he steps back and puts his hand on my shoulder and he sits down on the couch next to me. "That's not true," he says. "I really do think you're a force." And I can tell he's about to start getting sappy-snorty and I don't want that so I tell him it's fine.

Wendell bumps his paint-stained knee against mine and tells me that all this blending is hard for Bryce. As if it isn't for me. Then he gets up slowly and walks up the stairs. I can hear him knock quietly on Bryce's door.

It feels weird to be here without Mom. Like my team is down a player and when I look up I only see the other team's jerseys so I just have to contain and wait for the clock to run out.

The phone rings before I go upstairs. It's Grandma Bea. "Good day?" she asks.

I tell her about the girls on the soccer team list and how my teachers didn't let Bryce get away with being a bully-follower and that I found a new way to help Maximilian calm down if he gets stuck. I don't tell her about Aileyanna Absalon and how she thinks she's going to be number ten and play center midfield even though she's not because that's my position, because I know what Grandma would say. *Oh, quit that hogwash, Bea.*

"Sounds like a good day to me," she says. "You doing OK over there?"

"Yeah," I say. "I could use some M&M's, though."

She laughs and tells me to sleep tight.

That night I brush my teeth with the door closed and when I come out I can hear Wendell's voice in Bryce's room again. Cameron and Tucker are in there too now, like they're all having a late-game, time-out family huddle. I know Fred's in there, and Dodger and Roscoe are running up the stairs and pushing their way in through the door. Tucker looks out and sees me in my pajamas.

"You want to come in?" he asks.

Wendell calls, "Come on, Bea. We're just talking about school. Join us!" Bryce is sitting on his bed with his back to the door and maybe I'm making it up but his shoulders seem lower than I've seen them, like something heavy is pushing him down and making it hard to keep his head up, so I say it's OK and I'll see everyone tomorrow.

Wendell comes to the door and says, "You sure? You have everything you need? I can tell a pretty good mismatched animals story too, you know."

"I'm fine," I tell him even though I'm kind of mad that he knows about Mom's mismatched animals stories and then I'm mad that I'm mad about that.

"OK, sleep well," he says. "Waffles for breakfast? I unpacked the iron and I've got a new mix."

"Sure," I say. "Good night." But really I want to tell

him that he's trying too hard and it's making me feel like a guest and that I just want a bowl of Corn Pops.

Before I get in bed I try the walkie-talkie, even though I know it won't work. It doesn't.

I wake up early and no one's asking for my threes but I think to myself anyway: One, that my new teachers are cool. Two, school lunch isn't terrible. Three, girls' team.

I smell waffles and hear giggles from the kitchen as I'm getting dressed, and when I round the corner to the kitchen Wendell and Bryce are trying to catch the extra batter that's oozing out the front of the waffle iron. Bryce cups his hands while Wendell is searching for a dish towel. They're both laughing and Wendell's saying, "Guess I overloaded it, huh?" And I feel weird being here, like this is one of those in-between times and I shouldn't be peeking in. So I step back around the corner to the living room before they can see me.

But now I feel weird because I don't have anything to do in the living room so I just feel like a lurker-eavesdropper and I bet any second Cameron or Tucker will come bounding down the stairs and see me standing in the middle of the living room doing nothing. I pretend I'm looking for a book on the bookshelves. But even those aren't mine so I still feel awkward.

Cameron and Tucker are always reading and

yesterday after school they organized these shelves with all their favorites. I run my finger along the spines. Some are picture books and chapter books and some are young adult novels that are a hundred inches thick. They call these their "had to own it" shelves and they've been adding to it since they were in preschool. The bookshelves take up one whole wall and turn the corner to the next. We didn't have a "had to own it" shelf in the condo, but we visited the library every week.

I like reading too, but it's not easy for me, the way it seems to be easy for Cameron and Tucker and Maximilian. It's not that easy for Bryce either. I can tell.

They have a few Pete the Cat books on the shelves, which were my favorite. *Pete the Cat and His Four Groovy Buttons* was the first book Maximilian read to me when we were five and he'd figured out all the letter sounds and how they make words. We climbed the tree and sat on the big crooked "reading branch" and he pointed to each word as he read.

Cameron and Tucker also have a couple of Judy Moody books and *Diary of a Wimpy Kid* and *Shiloh*, which Maximilian read to me chapter by chapter in the tree and over the walkie-talkie after curfew.

Right as my finger gets to *Charlotte's Web* I smirk thinking about Fern's name and about Bryce being such a bully-follower and wonder if he figured out the pig's name like Ms. Kravitz told him too.

"You find something?"

Cameron's behind me and I kind of jump and pull out a book called *Bridge to Terabithia*. "Yeah," I say.

"Oh, that one," Cameron says, and puts his hand over his heart. "You can borrow it if you want."

"Thanks." I tuck it under my arm.

"Tissues," he says, pointing to the book. "You'll need tissues." Then he turns toward the kitchen. "I smell waffles."

There are two stacks of waffles in the middle of the counter and I'm wondering who eats that much breakfast, but before I can slide a stool around and grab a fork one whole stack is already gone and they're passing around butter and maple syrup. Then Tucker joins us and Wendell gives him his stool and stands between Bryce and the cabinets and we're all smushed in shoulder to shoulder. I tuck *Bridge to Terabithia* beneath my leg while I eat.

Mom comes home from her twenty-four-hour shift and drops her bag in the mudroom and Wendell gives her a hug. She kisses my forehead and asks us all how the first day went. Everyone says *good* or *fine* and asks about work and Wendell serves her a waffle and she and her belly squish in between Cameron and me. She links her arm through mine.

"Maybe we should've set the table," Wendell says.

"Nonsense," Mom says. "I like standing room only." When she finishes her waffle she says she's going to sleep for a few hours, then gives me a hug. "See you after school."

Then all the plates are in the sink and I rush back upstairs to get my backpack. I throw a pair of shorts, my cleats, and shin guards in my bag in case all Principal Meesley needed to do was check the list and practice starts today. And when I realize I'm still carrying *Bridge to Terabithia* I throw that in there too.

We don't line up outside with our teachers like we did yesterday. We know how to get from the bus to our classrooms already and that's fine with me because I want to stop by the office to knock on Principal Meesley's door. I want to know when practice is.

Ms. Landry is talking to a parent and Principal Meesley's door is closed.

"Not in yet," Ms. Landry says.

I huff a big, annoyed breath and head down the hall to Ms. Blaise and Ms. Kravitz's homeroom. Maximilian is waiting at our same table from yesterday. Aileyanna is putting her things in her cubby and Laurel and Georgia are calling, "A!" and tapping the space at their table like *come sit*.

She's wearing a pair of black pants that are cropped above the ankle with the same brown, flimsy boots, and a sweater that's shifted off one of her shoulders, showing a bright purple tank top strap and I can't tell if her shifted-sweater is on purpose and it's supposed to look like that or if she just leaned into her cubby wrong and it got all droopy.

Ms. Kravitz is squatting next to Kenny, Morris, and Bryce's table in the back talking about Wilbur, the pig in *Charlotte's Web*. "No more making fun of people's names. Not cool."

Maximilian types me a note on his graphing calculator and slides it over. *Bus OK?*

Yeah. Path OK? I slide it back.

Thumbs-up.

We've been passing notes this way ever since his grandparents got him a TI-84 for his birthday last year. It's what he asked for.

I'm wishing Principal Meesley would come in and announce the news that there will be a girls' team this year and tell us when practices start and who our coach is and when we're getting uniforms and that I'm number ten.

Ms. Blaise is calling for our attention and starting to explain a name game and I'm thinking what was all that talk about names yesterday if we still have to do an icebreaker name game today? And it's not even a fun one. It's the my-name-is-Ms.-Blaise-and-I-like-books one.

Then Ms. Blaise tosses a beach ball to Aileyanna. "My name is A and I like athletics."

Then she tosses the ball to me before I have a chance to think. "Bea," I say. "And I like . . ." I'm going through *B* words in my head but Ms. Blaise already said books and all I can think of is *boys* and *barf.* And for some reason I can't think of a single other *B* word in the whole English language. Boogers? Benadryl?

Ms. Kravitz tries to prompt me with a few ideas, but this isn't one of those times that I need extra help from a special teacher, this is just because nothing good starts with *B*. Band-Aids? Blisters?

"Bagels," I say. "I like bagels." And I guess I kind of do, but it's not like they're my favorite or anything.

"I would have said *bicycle kick* or *breakaway*," Aileyanna whispers to Laurel and Georgia, and she doesn't even really whisper it mean, but it still makes me want to bicycle kick a hard strike right smack into her thigh on a late-season cold day so the sting lasts.

"Those are good ones," Laurel whispers.

"Can you do a bicycle kick?" Georgia asks.

I don't hear Aileyanna's response because Maximilian has the beach ball and is saying he likes math, which is true, but Kenny and Morris are laughing and doing fake nerd snorts and when I whip around to glare at them, Bryce is shoving a pair of imaginary glasses up his nose.

Their laughter spreads to Mac and Wyatt at the table next to them and even up to Maddie and Tess and Quinn. It's not big all-out laughs. It's under their breath and behind their hands and I don't think Maximilian even notices so I don't know if I should tell them all to keep their mouths shut or just let it go.

Ms. Kravitz knows, though. "Math is an excellent thing to love, Maximilian," she says. Then she turns to Kenny and Morris and Bryce's table and asks, "Are you laughing because you think liking math is funny or boring or nerdy?"

Morris looks down at his hands. "N-no."

"I didn't even say anything," Kenny says.

Ms. Kravitz's still looking at them. "Well, I heard you laughing and I just wanted to check in about that because my name is Ms. Kravitz and I like kindness."

Someone says, *Ooooo*, and someone else says *burn*.

Ms. Kravitz motions for us to continue. Laurel likes lollipops and Fern likes Fridays and Kenny likes kites. Ms. Blaise says, "Lots of math goes into how kites fly," and winks at Kenny.

When it's Bryce's turn I can come up with a hundred things that start with *B*, of course. Brunch, beach, bed.

But Bryce takes forever thinking, then says, "Butterfingers."

The bell rings and Ms. Kravitz lines us up for our next class. The only period she doesn't come to is lunch. But I'll tell you one thing. I wish she would come to lunch with us, because today lunch is wild. I guess yesterday everyone was showing off their best behavior because it was the first day, but that's over. Way over.

No one's staying at their tables anymore and Principal Meesley is carrying a bullhorn and if he's too close to our table when he yells through it, Maximilian screams and covers his ears. And this year our lunch is a whole period later so I'm hungry and the line is long and we go up based on which class is the quietest so we'll probably never be first.

When I finish eating I dump my tray, push through a group of kids standing at the vending machine, and tap on Principal Meesley's shoulder.

"Find your seat," he says.

"I'm just wondering if practice . . ."

"Sit down!" he yells through the bullhorn and points to a group of eighth graders on the other side of the cafeteria.

Principal Meesley waves me off and starts dismissing our class to the playground for recess. We file out the door and Ms. Kravitz meets us out there with our recess aide, Mr. Duff, and everyone runs to different spots. Maddie and Fern are opening the big steel trunk under the eaves of the building and pulling out jump ropes. Laurel, Georgia, and Aileyanna go for the swings. Kenny and Morris put the lid down on the steel trunk and sit on top with their legs hanging over, banging their heels against the side and sighing and rolling their eyes whenever anyone wants to get a ball or Hula-Hoop from inside. Bryce follows them, banging his heels against the trunk too.

Maximilian and I run to the monkey bars. He starts to climb up and I think back to the summer he started teaching me the words to the Pete the Cat books on the reading branch and I taught him how to hang on and swing to the next bar. It was a good trade.

I start on one end and he starts on the other and we meet in the middle and try to pass each other without falling. We have this down. We both squish left and reach with our right arms and pass back-to-back to the next rung.

We do a couple more runs, then I see Aileyanna swing high, like really high, like I kind of think she might swing all the way up and over the top bar. She pumps her legs one more time and then, at the height of her arc, she jumps and flies and flies and lands on the heels of both her fancy brown boots.

"Whoa," Fern says and stops her jump roping.

"I can do that," Mac says and grabs the swing next to Aileyanna. Laurel and Georgia are pumping higher too and Wyatt takes the last swing. And before I can make it back across the monkey bars, everyone's pumping and jumping and flying but no one can stick the landing like Aileyanna.

"Let Bea try," Aileyanna says.

And to Mr. Duff and Ms. Kravitz it sounds like Aileyanna is "sharing and compromising well with her peers," which is a comment you can get on your report card, even though I never do. But really, I know what she's doing. She's looking me right in the eyes and it's a challenge. Can I fly as high as she does? Can I stick the landing? She's looking at me like this is going to decide who is center midfield. Who is number ten.

I roll up my Carhartts one more roll and kick off my flip-flops.

Swings aren't usually my thing. I get bored after ten seconds, but now I'm pumping hard and going as high as I can, until it feels like the swing is ready to dump me off. Then I use my arms and legs and abs to push off and fly and when I hit the ground I let my knees bend and hold on like I'm trying to contain a striker making a run up the midfield. And I stick the landing. And Maximilian cheers.

I give Aileyanna that look right back, the one that

says *I got this*. Then the bell rings and it's time to go inside so I slide back into my flip-flops and line up behind Ms. Kravitz.

In English class, Ms. Blaise gives us a tour of the library in the corner of her classroom. We all huddle in the rug area by the couch and the big chairs as she picks up one book after another and tells us a little about them. Sometimes she even reads the first page then puts it back in the bin. Everyone's reaching their arms out and saying *I want that one!*

"I'll tell you about more of my favorites tomorrow," she says, and then lets us explore the bins on our own.

I show Maximilian the book I took from Cameron and Tucker's "had to own it" shelves and he knows it immediately. "You think I can read this one?" I ask.

"I know you can."

And if Maximilian says I can, I can. He never lies.

"Want me to tell you anything about it?" he asks.

"No," I say, thumbing through the pages.

He starts to say that if I get stuck we can always go to the reading branch, but then he remembers. Remembers that I don't live there anymore. He can't just walk in my door and we can't just take off down the path. "We can check in at school about it," he says instead.

At the end of the day Principal Meesley comes in to make an announcement. He's holding the list. I slide to the edge of my seat and Aileyanna does too.

"The boys' team will begin practice tomorrow on Field A. Girls, you are welcome to join if you wish. There wasn't enough interest again this year."

"What?" I shout and stand straight up. "There are eleven names!"

Principal Meesley says if I have any questions I can find him later but I know what that means. I'll never find him. His office will be locked or he'll be busy yelling through some bullhorn.

"But read the list!" I continue.

"Bea," he says like that's final.

But it's not.

Then I see Aileyanna stand up. "Eleven is a team," she says.

Principal Meesley looks at Ms. Blaise and Ms. Kravitz like *I'm busy can you take care of this?* And they look right back at him like *They've got questions. You better have answers.*

Quinn stands up and says, "I signed up. I want to play."

"Like I said, you're welcome to join the boys if you want to try that."

Tess stands. "We don't want to join the boys anymore. We want our own team."

And if this were one of those sports movies that

92

Tucker always watches everyone would stand up one by one and demand a team and Meesley would have to give in. But instead he says, "You need a sub and a manager. That's thirteen. You have eleven. Sorry, girls."

He points to Kenny and Morris and Bryce and Mac and at some other boys in the room and says, "You can start calling me Coach. See you on Field A tomorrow." Then he leaves.

As soon as the door closes I look at Aileyanna and she looks back at me and this time it isn't a challenge kind of glare, it's a *now no one's going to be number ten* kind of glare, a *what are we going to do?* kind of glare.

I look at Ms. Blaise like *Can we?* And she looks at me like *You'd better.*

So I head out the door and down the hall and I know Aileyanna is right there next to me because the heels on her boots are clunking and I'm actually kind of glad because I'm mad and she's mad and even the click of her boot heels sounds mad and that feels kind of good.

"Hey!" I shout down the hall.

Principal Meesley stops outside his office. "Numbers are numbers," he says, then flips his sign so it reads *Do Not Disturb* and disappears inside.

8

MAXIMILIAN WALKS ME TO the bus after school and says
he's sorry about soccer and I wish I could just walk home
with him down our path to the condos, like we used to.
But instead he puts his hands on the sides of my shoulders and I say thanks then climb up the steps to the bus
back to Evergreen Road.

Aileyanna's in the first spot behind the bus driver
and instead of walking to the middle where I like to sit,
I throw my backpack in the seat across the aisle from
her and sit down.

"I can't believe you don't have a girls' soccer team
here," she says. "That doesn't even make sense. The
middle school where I would have gone in Brooklyn has
an A, B, and C team."

At first I want to say, yeah, that I can't believe it either, but the more she's talking about Brooklyn and all her soccer teams the more I'm wishing I had taken my seat in the middle.

"I would have been on the A team," she says and smiles. "Since I played all summer." Then she huffs a big sigh and asks, "What do girls even do here?"

And now I'm mad. Mad at Meesley, mad at Evergreen Road, mad at Brooklyn for having three soccer teams, mad at Aileyanna for coming to our town because it might not be Brooklyn but I actually kind of like it. And I'm thinking, *What do girls do here?* They prune apple trees and tap maples and learn CPR because the closest hospital is far. They wear pants that fit and sweatshirts that go over both shoulders and boots that can actually get muddy.

"You're the one who came here for a *quieter, slower life*," I say.

She raises up her eyebrows like she's trying to figure out where that came from and what the heck is wrong with me. But what the heck is wrong with me is that she thinks she can come here and be all MVG, and none of it even matters because Principal Meesley won't give either of us number ten on the boys' team anyway.

"Maybe you should've stayed in Brooklyn where all the soccer teams are."

Now her eyes turn down and she bites on her lip a little and I think she might even look like she's going to cry. Then she says, "Fine," and sits back hard against the seat and crosses her arms over her chest. I can't think of anything else to say and she's looking out the window now anyway so I turn toward my window too and we ride the rest of the way home like that, looking in opposite directions.

We get off at Evergreen and Bryce lingers with Morris while Aileyanna hurries off toward our houses and I do too. I'm keeping up with her fast-clacking boots and they sound mad again. She picks up the pace and so do I and I'm thinking we probably look like those professional racewalkers that Tucker made us watch in the last Summer Olympics.

We're both a little out of breath when we get to our houses. I turn left to go in my driveway and she turns right to go in hers and I'm fiddling with the garage code when I hear her strike a soccer ball against her fancy bounce-back net.

She's kicking hard. Nailing each ball with her instep then following through and landing square over her quad and the toe of her left brown boot. Like maybe she's mad at more than just Meesley. Or missing more than just her three soccer teams.

I watch her trap the ball. "Guess we'll be on the boys'

team then." She says it to the ball, but loud enough for me to hear.

Bryce is walking up the street now and I'm picturing playing on his team with Kenny and Morris and Mac and Wyatt and all the seventh- and eighth-grade boys who probably won't pass to me. It makes my hands clench into fists.

"No," I call across to Aileyanna's yard. Then I walk back to the end of my driveway. "We need to make a plan. This is some bullsharky."

She laughs when I say *bullsharky* but then she flips the ball up, sticks it beneath her arm, walks to the end of her driveway, and says, "I'm in." She pulls a cell phone from her pocket. "I'll text you after dinner. What's your number?"

I think of everything Mom tells me about cell phones. How they keep you from knocking on doors and looking into faces. And if there's one thing an Embers can do, it's knock on doors and look into faces. I roll my eyes when Mom tells me this stuff, but I say it to Aileyanna right now anyway. "I live right here. I'll just knock on your door."

She slides her phone back in her pocket and nods. A car passes on the road between us and Bryce is opening the door in the garage to let Dodger and Roscoe out and Cameron and Tucker are already inside.

I say "later" to Aileyanna and we both turn toward our houses. Before I get to the garage I'm thinking I'm going to ask my mom about a cell phone again because if Aileyanna has one, why shouldn't I?

Mom is hanging one of the Valentines' paintings above the couch. She has a hammer stuck in the elastic waist of her maternity pants and a nail between her teeth.

"Hey, kids!" she lisps around the nail. "Is this straight?"

And I'm wondering if she means kids like *her* kids, like we're all her kids now because they got married and we live together, or if she's just saying kids because we're all under eighteen.

Tucker rushes over and grabs the frame from her. "Here, I'll hold it. You look."

She steps back between Cameron and me. "Down an inch." Then she hands Tucker the hammer and nail and he makes a little mark on the wall and hangs the painting.

Bryce comes back in with the dogs and Cameron starts digging through the cabinets for snacks and Mom pulls me down on the couch and says, "How's middle school?"

I'm telling her about Principal Meesley and how he said eleven isn't enough and Mom slams her thigh with her open hand and says, "No!" And I want to tell her about Aileyanna and how she seems kind of show-offy with her Brooklyn clothes and jumping off swings and thinking she's going to be number ten, but Bryce is in the kitchen, elbow-deep in a huge, family value bag of chips, and I'm sure he's listening to everything I'm saying.

"So what happens next?" Mom asks.

I shrug because I don't really want to tell her I'm going to Aileyanna's after dinner to figure out a plan. I don't want her to get all excited about me making a new friend, because it's not like that.

But then big-mouth Bryce crunches another fistful of chips and says, "So are you and A like friends now? I saw you talking outside."

I give him a scowl.

"Is that the girl from across the road?" Mom asks.

"Yeah. She signed up for soccer too," I tell her. "I'm going over after dinner to figure out how to get a manager and one more player. That's it, though."

Mom gives me a nod and Bryce says, "She seems nice."

I shoot back, "You also think Kenny and Morris are nice."

"They are," he says.

"To who?"

"OK, you two." Mom cuts us off, and Bryce leaves

the chips open on the counter, picks up Fred, and heads upstairs to his room.

Cameron and Tucker sit at two of the kitchen stools and Cameron's talking about an assignment that he thinks is totally unfair. "It's for Behavioral Science," he says. "It's supposed to be an easy A class, but then Ms. Greggs tells us today that we each have to take a two-day turn with this fake baby doll thing that cries all the time."

I laugh and ask what that has to do with school and Cameron tells me that they're studying something called development, which is basically how our brains grow, and there's a whole unit on infants and their needs. "They lock this key around our wrist that you have to hold in the doll's back in the right position depending on what it needs, like a new diaper or a bottle or something."

"Ha!" Mom says. "I wish it worked like that! Believe me, real babies don't come with some magical key."

Tucker says, "Just put it in the basement under a bunch of blankets or something. I mean, it's not like it's real."

I'm thinking that's a good idea, but Cameron explains that the doll has a computer in it that records all the stuff you do and don't do. Like if it gets shaken, or how long it takes you to get it to stop crying.

"Give the key to some girl who wants to babysit," Tucker says.

Cameron shakes his head. "They lock it on you with this special zip tie thing that comes with the doll and if it's cut, you fail."

Mom laughs again and says, "Well, you'll have to figure it out then."

"I'm a swimmer, though," he says. "I can't take a fake baby to morning practice and have it crying on the deck. Plus, I have a bunch of college visits coming up and there's no way I'm taking some doll to an interview."

Mom rubs her belly. "Well, you'll be all trained and certified for your baby sibling."

Wendell comes home and we have dinner around the big table in our same seats. Cameron tells Wendell and Bryce what he told us about his Behavioral Science assignment and Bryce can't stop cracking up and Wendell says, "You have a point, you can't take a crying fake baby to a college interview."

Mom cuts right in, "What do you mean he can't? He certainly can."

"It's not real, Louise. What's he going to do? Introduce the doll to the Stanford recruiter who has flown across the country to see him swim, then ask him to hold it while he shows off his butterfly in the pool with a key flapping off his wrist?"

We all laugh at the image, but Mom says, "If that's what he has to do, then yes."

Wendell gives her a look like *You're kidding right?* and she gives him one back that says *Not even a little bit* and we all get quiet.

"I think Ms. Greggs is trying to teach them responsibility," Mom says.

Then Wendell looks down at his plate and shakes his head. "The boys understand responsibility. Too much. I just want him to go to swim practice and have a college interview without a baby in his arms."

For a second I think my mom is going to fire back because she's an Embers. But instead she looks him right in his eyes, and says, "I didn't mean . . ."

"It's fine." And I know Wendell wants to move on and have everything be OK and not think about how Cameron and Tucker know a lot about raising a baby already. A real baby, their baby brother. And he didn't come with a magical key.

Mom shifts her weight and takes a deep breath and I can tell the baby's kicking her. I can even see its little foot moving under Mom's stretchy top. Wendell raises his eyebrows. "Everything all right?"

"Yeah," Mom says and rubs her belly. "Just feisty and wants in on this conversation, seeing as how they're the actual baby of the family."

That makes everyone laugh and start talking about other things and eating again.

After we clear the table and fill the dishwasher I tell Mom I'm going to Aileyanna's to make a plan. She puts her arms on my shoulders and says OK. Wendell has a hundred questions but Mom says she'll fill him in on all the soccer news later and I pull on a sweatshirt and my sneakers and head out.

I knock on Aileyanna's door and her mom answers and welcomes me in and she seems nice now even though she stopped me from shoving Morris at the bus stop. I take off my shoes and say, "Thanks for having me over," and the whole time I'm wishing I had just walked twenty-eight steps to Maximilian's condo where I don't ever have to knock or thank his grandparents for having me over because they always say *Mi casa es tu casa* and Mom always says the same thing to Maximilian and that means that we can come and go and eat whatever we want from any of the cabinets.

Her mom calls Aileyanna and she comes downstairs. "Hey."

"Hey," I say.

I follow her to the kitchen where there are two stools. She sits on one of them and pulls over a notebook. "Let's make the list first," she says. She writes *Girls' Team* on the top and then *A Absalon* because it seems like she always has to be first. She slides the notebook over to me and I'm thinking of writing my name above hers, but

I can hear Grandma's voice saying, *Quit that hogwash, Bea* so I just forget it and add *Bea Embers* to the list.

"You know the rest?" she asks. "There's Georgia from our class, and Tess, and who else?"

I remember all eleven because I've known some since kindergarten and because I can still see their names written on the soccer sign-ups, before Principal Meesley folded it up and stuffed it in his pocket.

Girls' Team
A Absalon
Bea Embers
Georgia Ludlow
Quinn Williams
Fern Mandly
Tess Rogers
Emmie Powers
Jamie Burgos
Nelle Emerson
Micah Bond
Cara Elroy

We look over the list. "OK, we just need to get two more girls," A says. "And one of them doesn't even have to play. They just have to write down numbers and make sure all our soccer balls are accounted for at the end of practice."

"I don't know why we have to have a manager," I say. "I swear Meesley's just trying to make it impossible."

"He's the worst."

"You don't even know."

"Is there anyone who's not already on the list that we can call to convince?" she asks. Her cell phone is next to her on the counter and she taps her fingers on it. The screen lights up to show a picture of her and her mom in the background.

I scan the eleven names. All the girls from rec last year are on the list and Georgia told me that all the seventh and eighth graders who quit the boys' team last year signed up too. I'm trying to think of any other girls in our school who might join the team and it's harder than coming up with things that start with *B*.

"You can't think of anyone?" she asks.

"Not really."

Her phone vibrates and I look over at the screen. It says *Dad* and Aileyanna presses *Decline*.

"Then we need to go around school and ask people to sign up until we get two more," she says.

"Tomorrow morning," I tell her, because we can't waste any time with someone like Meesley.

Her mom, who is in the other room typing on her computer, looks up and says, "I can drive you early if you want so you can catch kids coming off the buses."

"I can be here at seven forty-five," I say. "If that's OK."

"You're welcome anytime, Bea," her mom says and smiles. And that's not the same as *Mi casa es tu casa* but it feels nice. On the way out I see one of those professional pictures of Aileyanna. She looks a lot younger and is kneeling in her soccer uniform with a ball under her arm. Number ten.

"I've been number ten since third grade," she tells me.

"I have since second," I tell her even though it's not true. We didn't actually get numbers until fourth grade. But I don't want her thinking that she can move to my town and keep her number. That's not how it works.

9

THE NEXT MORNING GRANDMA Bea calls for my threes and then asks, "You getting enough elbow room, Bea?"

It's hard to hear her because Bryce is making a big deal about starting soccer today. He's parading around the living room with his stinky shin guards and pretending there's a ball at his feet that he's kicking through Dodger's legs. "Bryce Valentine! MVP!"

I press the phone to my ear and say, "I'm working on it, Grandma."

And I'll tell you one thing. What I really want to do is steal Bryce's invisible ball and tell him to cut it out. And I want to tell Grandma that no, I don't have enough elbow room because Bryce Valentine is in my class, and on my bus, and lives in my house, and if we don't find two more girls this morning, he'll be on my soccer team too. And that's not enough elbow room for anyone.

"I got this," I tell her.

"I know you do, Bea," she says.

Aileyanna's mom drops us off in the circle outside of school and we wait on a bench for the buses to pull up. I have the list and a pen in my hand and I'm ready to write down the names of the first two girls who say OK.

I'm flipping the pen around through my fingers and Aileyanna's swinging her legs and letting her feet scuff the pavement. "How long have you been playing?" she asks.

"Forever."

"Me too," she says. "My dad taught me how to dribble in the park across from our apartment before I started preschool." She's looking down at her swinging feet. "He still lives there, but it's not a park anymore."

I don't know if I should say sorry. About how her dad's still there. Or how the park isn't.

"My mom and my grandma Bea and aunt Tam taught me how to play in the yard behind my condo," I tell her. Thinking back makes my heart ache a beat because now I'm wondering who's sitting on our stools and sleeping in my room and if they've met Aunt Tam. "But we were always all on the same team," I tell her. I laugh a little remembering it. "We always passed to each other and made our way across the yard to the two sweatshirts we threw down for goalposts. No defense. No goalie. Just the four of us working it up the field together."

"Same with my dad and me." She says it like a whisper, like maybe her heart might have ached a beat with remembering too. "We were like that. On the same team."

The first bus pulls up, then another behind that, and kids start streaming off and hurrying toward the double doors of the main entrance. Aileyanna and I look at each other. "Split up?" she asks. "Or double team?"

"Double team," I say, and we take off together toward the mob coming off the front bus.

The first girl we see is Beth Winters, a seventh grader from another class and she says she can't play because she works for her grandpa at the country store after school.

She walks toward a group of friends from her class and we follow her. When we ask about soccer they all say, "No thanks," and walk off.

Then we see Emmie, who's number seven on our list. She tells us Principal Meesley came to their class yesterday too and there's no way she's playing for the boys' team again. "He puts you in for like three minutes at the end of the game, if they're winning, and then says things like, *Good effort, men!* And I'm like *Helloooo?*"

"That's why we're trying to find two more girls," I tell her.

She links arms with Aileyanna and me and steers us in the direction of the next bus pulling up. "I'll come with you."

We see Georgia from our class and then Quinn and Fern and Tess and before the bell rings all eleven of us from the list are walking together, some of us linked arm in arm, trying to get two more girls to team up with us.

Everyone we talk to either already has something they have to do after school, or has never played soccer before and doesn't want to start something new and when we say, *Not even manager?* they shake their heads.

We move from bus to bus, group to group, with no luck, and the bell is ringing for us to get to our homerooms. We stop by the flagpole and huddle up and some of the girls are starting to talk about whether they're going to show up for the boys' team practice after school today or not and most everyone is shaking their heads and saying *forget it.*

But then Aileyanna pushes to the middle and clears her voice. "No, we can't forget it," she says. "We deserve a team. Make an announcement in your homerooms. We will too. Keep asking until you've asked every girl twice."

That gets everyone saying *Yeah!* and *OK!* and I'm thinking that Aileyanna is already starting to feel like the captain of this team and that's not how this is supposed to go. So before I even know I'm doing it, I stick my hand to the middle and call for everyone to *bring it in.* "Team on three!" I say, and when I get to three, eleven voices blend together and raise up for *Team!*

We leave the huddle and all start moving toward the middle school wing and I see Kenny and Morris in the hallway, putting their hands together and mocking *Team!* in high, squeaky voices as they walk toward Ms. Blaise and Ms. Kravitz's room, and I want to squash them with a pair of mud-caked cleats because I had all this good feeling in me and they ruined it with their stupid little giggles. But Aileyanna is there and Quinn and Georgia and Fern and Tess and with the six of us walking down the hall toward homeroom together, the good feeling comes back. A feeling like maybe we can do this. Find two more and keep our team.

When we get to homeroom, I sit down next to Maximilian and he passes me his TI-84 calculator.

Team?

Not yet.

He gives me a nervous look.

Then Aileyanna is raising her hand and asking Ms. Blaise if she can make an announcement. Ms. Blaise says OK and the class quiets and Aileyanna stands up and I do too because it's not just her announcement.

"We need two more girls for the soccer team," I say quickly. I look around and my eyes stop on Maddie and then Laurel because their names aren't on the list.

"Yeah," Aileyanna takes over. "Even though we have a full team Principal Meesley says we need a sub and a manager. He thinks we're just going to give up. But we're not."

Aileyanna's on a roll and she's sounding like a captain again, like the captain for the US Women's National Team up there, like Megan Rapinoe getting everyone pumped to stand up to Meesley and tell him that this is all some big, big bullsharky.

"It would be this school's first-ever girls' team," Aileyanna continues. "So you'd be making history!"

That gets Maddie scooching forward in her seat a little bit, but still no hands go up. So Aileyanna leans in and tries to make eye contact. Laurel looks away and Maddie mouths *Sorry*.

"Just think about it," she says. Then sits down.

"You can sign up with me," I say, and wave the list.

Maximilian slides his TI-84 back across the table to me.

That was good.

The bell rings but we have English first period so

Ms. Blaise starts talking about reading and how she loves going to the library to choose a stack of books, and how she tries to really picture the story in her brain as she reads. She holds up a few books she finished over the summer. Then she says that she's going to give us time to read in class every day. Whatever we want.

"Whatever we want?" Wyatt calls out.

"Whatever you want," Ms. Blaise repeats.

Mac pulls a *Sports Illustrated Kids* magazine from his backpack and holds it up. "Anything?"

"Anything," Ms. Kravitz says. "I already read that issue. It's great."

"You did?"

She nods and Ms. Blaise lays out some ground rules. First, we have to be reading something we *want* to be reading. Second, we have to find a place in the room that helps us focus on our reading. Third, we have to respect other people's reading choices and places.

"Seriously?" Wyatt asks. "You're not going to give us a list we have to read or anything?"

"Seriously," Ms. Blaise says. "We want you to create your own lists."

For a few minutes it feels like this plan will never work because everyone is super loud, looking for books, moving tables, finding places to stretch out on the floor. But Ms. Blaise isn't trying to shush anyone yet, and she's even adding to the excitement, helping kids pick books they might enjoy from the classroom library bins.

Maximilian doesn't like the noise and disorder, though. I can tell because he already has his book, he always has a book, and he's ready to read and he's starting to shake his head back and forth like maybe he can sweep all the commotion away.

Before I can find the spot between his thumb and pointer finger or start counting with him by eights, Ms. Kravitz is there and she's asking if he'd like to come with her outside for just a moment. She doesn't say it like he's in trouble, though, she says it like she's trying to help. He nods and leaves with her.

I pull *Bridge to Terabithia* out of my backpack and look at the cover. There's a big tree and two kids on the front. The tree has huge roots and rocks at its base, just like Maximilian's and my climbing tree behind the condo, and if it had a stamped-down path and couple of lower branches to swing up on, it'd look exactly like it.

Little by little the room is getting quieter and before I flip to the first page, it's silent. Aileyanna is sitting on a pillow, tucked in the corner of the library space. Mac and Wyatt are reading their magazines on the couch. Kenny is still at his table with a pile of graphic novels stacked next to him. He's looking carefully at each comic frame and turning the pages slowly. Bryce pulls a book from his backpack and I wonder if he got it from Cameron and Tucker's shelves. He unfolds a camping chair on the floor and opens to the first page.

Then the door creaks open and Maximilian comes back in. He sits down and whispers, "I've already read two pages with Ms. Kravitz." Then he turns to page three.

I start reading too and Ms. Kravitz sits down with a camping chair next to Bryce and pulls out an iPad. They have a quick whisper-conversation and she shows him something on the screen and says, "Give it a try."

Then she leaves him with the iPad and goes to sit with Fern and Maddie, who have a pile of picture books on the table between them. She motions for them to come with her and they go into the little office space in the back of the room. I can hear through the door that they're reading aloud, in quiet voices.

Ms. Blaise finishes checking in with Morris, who's reading the second book in the Percy Jackson series, and then she settles in to a spot near the front of the room and pulls out a skinny book called *From the Notebooks of Melanin Sun*, and reads.

I read the whole first chapter of *Bridge to Terabithia* about a boy named Jess Aarons and how quickly he can run and how he wants to be the fastest kid in the fifth grade. He has four sisters and he's trying to sneak out early in the morning without anyone waking up so he can go run across the cow field, and I don't blame him one bit. In fact, I actually start to really hope he makes it out there, past his sleeping family, just to get a little bit of elbow room.

Just as Jess crouches down and takes off to run like the wind there's a knock at the classroom door. And I'll tell you one thing. That's never happened to me before, where I forgot I was in school because I was running around the cow field with some character in a book.

Principal Meesley comes in and of course he would interrupt right now, because when I look up I notice I'm not the only who forgot they were in school for a minute. He looks at Ms. Blaise like *What on Earth is going on in here?* And *Why are you just sitting there and not teaching?* But Ms. Blaise shoots him a look back like *You don't know a thing about what's going on in here so you best stop before you start.*

"A minute," he says, and he doesn't even whisper.

Ms. Blaise joins him just outside the classroom and I can't hear everything they're saying, but I think Principal Meesley says *Just do what you can.* And I know I hear Ms. Blaise say something back but I can't tell what, and then I hear his squeaky footsteps down the hall.

I catch eyes with Aileyanna and Georgia and Quinn and Tess and I know we're all wondering the same thing.

If any of that was about our soccer team. But when she comes back in the room Ms. Blaise just sits and opens her book again.

Ms. Kravitz comes out from the little office room, but Fern and Maddie stay in there, trading picture books. She says in a loud whisper to the whole class, "We're going to read for another ten minutes," and everyone groans. But it's not a groan like they're so bummed we have to keep reading for ten more minutes. It's a groan like they can't believe we're only getting ten more minutes and no one wants to stop.

Then she sits down next to me and asks me how I chose my book. I mean to just shrug my shoulders and say I liked the cover, but before I know it I'm telling her about Cameron and Tucker's "had to own it" shelves and how Cameron and Tucker are Bryce's brothers, not mine, but we all have to live together because their dad married my mom. I tell her I was just looking at the books on their shelves, and I found this one. And then I tell her that Maximilian taught me how to read in a tree that looks kind of like the one on the cover.

Ms. Kravitz nods. "Well, that's as good a way to find a book as any," she says. "What do you know so far?" She taps the cover of *Bridge to Terabithia*.

I tell her not much. That I know Jess Aarons wants to be the fastest kid in the grade, and that his house is full of too many sisters. "And I just read that there's a U-Haul truck moving a family in next to him too." I'm thinking about Aileyanna moving in across the road and wondering if the family in the book will have a kid too. I bet so.

Ms. Kravitz smiles and says, "Great reading. I'll check in with you tomorrow to see if you find out any more."

Class is over and everyone whines, "One more page!" And Ms. Blaise says if we borrowed a book from her library we can take it home with us if we want. There are a couple of little squeals and everyone's zipping up their backpacks when she calls for our attention.

"Also, Principal Meesley just informed me that we'll have a new student in our class beginning tomorrow. A sixth grader. She's getting a tour of the school right now and may join us in the afternoon for homeroom just to say hi."

I look at Aileyanna and I know she's thinking what I'm thinking. Maybe the new girl plays soccer.

We all keep packing our backpacks, but Ms. Blaise claps her hands three times. "Listen for one minute," she says. "The new student is coming from a school that doesn't have a class like ours, one with two teachers and a group of students who are exceptional and welcoming. She'll be coming with an interpreter too," Ms. Blaise says. "Because she is deaf and communicates using American Sign Language."

A few kids say, "What?"

Ms. Kravitz explains to us that she was born unable to hear with her ears, and because of that, she learned a different language, one you speak with your hands, one you can see.

"Cool," says Tess.

I feel really stupid for wondering if she can play soccer, I mean, without being able to hear, but that's what I'm wondering when Kenny flutters his hands in front of Morris's face and they both crack up.

I'm thinking Ms. Blaise is going to shoot them down, but instead she looks right at Bryce, who is sitting next to them and says, "Thank you, Bryce, for not laughing at our new student and her unique abilities."

And I can't believe it. If she had given Bryce one more second he would have laughed right along with them, but instead, she's giving him a compliment and acting like he's such an example. And I can't actually believe that I can't believe it, because Bryce Valentine gets away with everything.

Ms. Kravitz lines us up for our next class. Aileyanna is first in line, of course, but I'm right behind her and Fern comes up behind us and whispers, "I talked to Maddie about the team while we were reading and she can't because she has to pick up her little brothers after school and take care of them until her mom comes home."

"Bummer," I say.

Then as we're walking down the hall I see the other classes lined up and when I find Emmie and Micah at the back of the lines they both look at me and shake their heads. No luck. We're still at eleven girls.

10

OUR CLASS GETS IN trouble a hundred times throughout the rest of the day. Mostly because we get caught reading under our desks in other classes and every time that happens Ms. Kravitz tells us we have to put our books away, but she says it with this little smile that makes us think she's maybe a tiny bit happy about our sneak-reading.

We're also getting in trouble because all the girls can't stop talking about soccer. Our time's almost up and as soon as the end-of-day bell rings, the boys' team will change into their gear and run out to Field A behind the school and we'll have to decide if we're running with them or sitting out the season.

I try again to convince Laurel but she doesn't change her mind. "Sorry."

"Not even manager?" I ask.

"Definitely not."

"It's OK," I tell her, because it's not her fault we won't have a team. It's Meesley's.

Our math teacher, Mr. Henny, is drawing a number line across the white board and Maximilian is copying it down in his graph paper notebook. He's also graphing equations on his TI-84 for fun because Mr. Henny isn't moving quickly enough for him. He slides his calculator over to me.

Shhhh.

It makes me laugh because he's the only person who would ever use a TI-84 calculator to tell his friend to shut her mouth during math class because he didn't want to miss counting down the number line.

Then it hits me. Maximilian. He could be our manager. Who cares if he's not a girl. It's not like he's going to be on the field. He'd be sitting on the sideline counting and recording and he could even use his TI-84 and graph paper notebook if he wanted.

Will YOU be our manager? Lots of counting. Math. I slide the calculator over to him.

He taps the eraser of his pencil four times perfectly in the middle of a square on his notebook. I know what he's thinking. He's not one for groups. He's not one for after school. School's enough.

I take the TI-84 back and type in, *I'm not sure any-one else could count high enough to record all our goals.*

He laughs a little and I type more. *I promise we'll try to score an even amount of goals every game.*

He smiles and rolls his eyes at me.

Please.

He taps his eraser four more times.

OK.

I jump up and press my hands on both his shoulders and say "thank you" and I don't even care that it's the middle of math class and that Mr. Henny caps his white board marker, again, and stares at me.

"What is going on today?" he asks. Then he leans against the board and accidentally erases from negative two all the way to positive one on his number line with the back of his shirt.

"We're trying to make a girls' soccer team," I tell him. "And we're really close."

He nods and says, "Well, that certainly is excit-ing." And I think he's going to say *But can't this wait until after class?* because that's what teachers say about really important stuff, and I'm ready to say, *no actually, it can't.* But instead he says, "So what do you need?"

I tell him about the eleven girls who signed up and what Principal Meesley said about a sub and a man-ager. Mr. Henny turns around and points to eleven on the number line. Then makes two big arcing bumps with his marker to thirteen.

Maximilian stands up and says, "Except I've just agreed to be their manager because I have outstanding skills in math."

Kenny snickers and Morris mumbles, "For the *girls'* team?"

But Maximilian just answers him back straight, "Yes, for the girls' team." And even if that makes them snicker more, Aileyanna and Georgia and Quinn and Tess and Fern all pump their fists and say "yes!" and that makes Maximilian smile. Then he takes a funny little bow and sits back down.

Mr. Henny says, "Sweet!" and bumps his marker from eleven to twelve and makes a point. "One more to go," he says.

On our way back to homeroom at the end of the day we see the other classes in the hall again and we tell Emmie about Maximilian. She goes to give him a high five, but I tell her he doesn't do high fives.

"I do these," he says, and puts out his fist.

They connect knuckles and laugh and Emmie says, "Maybe Meesley will let us play with eleven plus a manager?"

But we all know Principal Meesley. So we all know he won't.

When we get back to homeroom Ms. Blaise is sitting at a table with the new girl and two other grown-ups. The girl's hands are flying one hundred miles per hour and she's not just using her hands, she's using her whole face and her whole body. One of the grown-ups smiles and the other must be the interpreter because she speaks out loud to Ms. Blaise, telling her what the girl just said.

"I'm already reading a book I really like. It's called *The Watsons Go to Birmingham—1963*," she says.

"Wonderful," Ms. Blaise replies, and the interpreter puts up her hands, palms out toward the girl, then moves them down. *Wonderful.*

We all go in to take our seats and the four of them stand. The new girl hardly comes to Ms. Blaise's shoulder. She's short and skinny and wears glasses and braces and little kid jeans with hearts embroidered all the way down and looks more like she's in fourth grade than sixth. And I wonder what it must be like to see us all coming in, zipping up our sweatshirts and our backpacks, our mouths moving, but not be able to hear what we're saying. I wonder if it's just silent, or if it sounds like we're mumbling, like when you're underwater, or if there's some kind of background sound like a mosquito buzzing by your ear.

Then I see that Ms. Blaise is pointing to Aileyanna and me and the new girl smiles and walks right over to us, and I'm expecting her to be nervous because she looks like she'd be shy, but she's not nervous at all. She waves her hand in a salute and the interpreter says, "Hi."

I say hi back which immediately makes me feel stupid because I know she can't hear me. The interpreter does the wave-salute back to her, but the girl is watching my lips instead of the interpreter and I think she could see the *hi* there because she smiles. Then her hands start moving quickly and easily and her interpreter tells us what she's saying.

"Ms. Blaise told me you're starting a girls' soccer team. I can play."

We all scream and she can definitely see that because she starts jumping up and down.

Ms. Kravitz is introducing the new girl to the class but I can't pay attention because my heart is beating *team-team team-team team-team* and I can't wait to find the girls from the other classes and I can't wait to storm Field A and ask Principal Meesley when our practices start.

The bell rings and we all run out the door, the new girl and her interpreter and Maximilian too, and when we see Emmie and Micah in the hallway I say, "We have a team!" and lift the new girl's arm in the air like she's just won a wrestling match.

The interpreter is signing everything we're saying,

126

which is mostly just *Yes!* and *Whoo-hoo!*

Then Emmie whispers to Aileyanna and me, "Who is that? Is she new?" And I realize we were too excited and never even learned her name.

Aileyanna puts her hand out toward the new girl and says, "I'm A."

I reach out and say, "I'm Bea."

The girl shakes our hands and the interpreter holds up her fist, a strong, tight, powerful-looking sign, for *A*. Then she points to me and flattens her hand and tucks her thumb across her palm like it's hiding, for the letter *B*. I'm thinking, of course Aileyanna even gets a cooler sign.

The girl smiles and gives that hi salute again. Then she points to herself and I watch the fingers on her right hand fly. Then both her hands start moving together and stop in the curved *C* shape, twice.

The interpreter says, "My name is Cecelia Munroe, but everybody calls me Cece."

Cece laughs and points to Aileyanna and gives that powerful-fist sign. Then she points to me and makes the flat-hand-thumb-hiding sign. Then she points to herself and holds up her double-pulsed-*C* sign.

The interpreter smiles and says, "A. B. Cece."

11

PRINCIPAL MEESLEY IS SETTING up bright orange cones on Field A and the boys' team is sitting in a circle, with Bryce in the middle leading stretches. Principal Meesley probably saw that he got rec soccer MVP last year and made him captain on the first day. Bet he didn't see his championship-stealing offside goal.

We're walking across the field, all of us, the whole girls' team, and a couple of the boys start looking up and pointing. "Coach!" Wyatt yells and Principal Meesley stops what he's doing.

When we reach the eighteen-yard line where Principal Meesley is standing he shakes his head and says, "Are you all really joining the boys? With a team this big, you won't get much playing time."

"No," I say.

The interpreter signs *no* by closing her first two fingers and thumb together in a way that really looks like a *no*.

"We're our own team," I say. "Twelve players and a manager."

The interpreter signs *team* with two fists. She tucks her thumbs under her pointer fingers and moves both fists out and around in a big circle and closes them hard for *team*.

He starts counting us and when he gets to Maximilian he stops. "Maximilian?"

"I'm the manager," he says. "For the girls."

Principal Meesley lets out a little laugh and Kenny and Morris follow him and then Bryce follows them until most of the boys' team is cracking up. And I feel a fire in my gut because they might all cling together like little molecules, but we can too. Before I can even think of what to say back to all their laughing I can hear Ms. Kravitz's voice in my head.

"What's so funny?" I ask Meesley. "I hear you laughing so I want to check in about that. Do you think it's funny that Maximilian, who is very organized and excellent at math, is our manager?"

Principal Meesley looks at me like I better hold my tongue, but I won't.

And neither will Aileyanna because she steps up right next to me and says, "You told us twelve players and a manager. Here we are. When do we start?"

He takes a breath. "It's not that easy, girls. There's a registration fee for entering you in the league and getting a coach costs money too and if you aren't serious then it's not worth—"

"We are serious," Tess cuts in.

He raises his eyebrows at her. "You've already quit once before," he says.

"I quit the *boys'* team," she responds.

"I have practice right now, girls. We'll have to talk about this another time." He starts laying down the rest of the orange cones.

All the boys stand up, some still laughing, and start dribbling balls in the coned-in area. "Quick feet!" Meesley yells.

Then Emmie steps up and so does Micah and Quinn, and then Georgia and Nelle too. "But—"

He blows his whistle, drowning out our voices.

Then Cece reaches up and taps him on his shoulder. Her hands make three clear signs. The interpreter stands next to her and says the words slowly, just the way Cece signed them. "We. Aren't. Disappearing."

And the whole team says, "Yeah!"

"You'll miss your bus," Meesley says and nods

toward the school. "Go on."

We tell him we'll be back tomorrow, with our gear. Then we all turn and walk together to catch our buses and we say bye to Cece and the interpreter and her mom, who was waiting outside the school with Ms. Blaise and Ms. Kravitz. And I give Maximilian a fist bump and tell him thanks again. He takes off across the field and into the woods, onto our old path, past our tree, and home to the condos.

When I get on the bus, I sit across the aisle from Aileyanna again. I have the list in my hands and I take a pen from my backpack and write in the last two names.

A Absalon
Bea Embers
Georgia Ludlow
Quinn Williams
Fern Mandly
Tess Rogers
Emmie Powers
Jamie Burgos
Nelle Emerson
Micah Bond
Cara Elroy
Cece Munroe
Manager: Maximilian Lee

"Meesley better get us a coach and a schedule and some uniforms right away," I say.

"Knock on his door tomorrow before school?" Aileyanna asks.

I nod my head. "And at lunch too. And recess. And whenever we walk past on our way to the bathroom."

"Until he says OK," she says.

"It's a plan."

We don't say anything the rest of the ride and we don't do the awkward racewalk thing down Evergreen Road that we did yesterday. It's a little windy so I zip up my sweatshirt and she pulls the two sides of her sweater together and ties the band of it around her waist in a bow. The sweater's as long as a dress, which seems like it would be annoying, annoying like a dress.

We're almost back at our houses when she says, "So what's it like living with Bryce? Is that weird?"

At first I want to tell her it's none of her business, but instead I say, "Super weird."

"I bet," she says.

"And it's not just him," I tell her. "It's his two older brothers, his dad, his two dogs, his cat, and all the weird stuff I know that I feel like I shouldn't know."

"Like what?" she asks.

"Like what color his toothbrush is."

"Super weird," she says.

We reach our driveways and I say, "Yeah, it was better when it was just my mom and me."

Aileyanna nods and looks down at the ground and I'm thinking I should ask her a question too so I say, "What happened to the park by your old apartment?"

"Swanky new building," she says, and even though I don't know exactly what *swanky* means I can tell it's not as cool as a park with soccer fields. She pulls the band of her sweater tighter around her waist, says she'll see me tomorrow, and turns up her driveway.

Just as I'm about to punch in the garage code I hear her call, "Bea! What color's his toothbrush?"

I smile and yell, "Purple! With glitter stars!" We both laugh and wave bye and head into our houses.

Mom is in the living room doing exercises on the floor that I think might be yoga. I sit down on the rug next to her.

"You're not at soccer practice," she says. "That's not a good sign." She drops her position and sits down cross-legged on the rug next to me. Her belly swells out toward her lap. "Tell me."

"We got another player to sign up and Maximilian is going to be our manager."

"Oh, Maximilian!" Mom says. "That's so perfect."

"But Principal Meesley says we'll have to talk about it another time. Like it still might not happen even though we did what he said."

She shakes her head and says *Uh-oh* and I'm thinking she's talking about Meesley but then she grabs her belly and closes her eyes.

"Mom?"

Cameron and Tucker come in the door laughing at something and Mom takes a big huffing breath and opens her eyes.

"Mom?"

"I'm OK," she says, but then she closes her eyes again and breathes and I move closer to her and put my hand on her back.

Cameron and Tucker put their bags down. "Louise?"

The baby's not due for five more weeks so I know it can't be time. But Mom says in a steady voice, "Cameron, my keys are on the counter. I think I'm going to have you drive me to the doctor. Just in case. I'm sure it's nothing."

My heart starts to beat fast and I can feel the blood pumping through my ears. "I'm coming too," I say.

"Me too," says Tucker. He helps Mom up and Cameron runs to the car and opens the passenger door.

Tucker and I get in the back and everyone buckles up and Cameron starts the car and reverses fast out of the driveway.

"Cameron!" Mom says. "You are *not* an ambulance driver."

That makes us all laugh and I feel a little better just hearing my mom being my mom, even if she's breathing all gaspy and huffy.

Tucker takes out his cell phone and calls Wendell. "He'll get Bryce and meet us there," he says.

When we get to the hospital, Cameron drops us off and goes to park the car. "Meet us in Labor and Delivery," Mom says.

"But it's too early, Mom. Right?" I say.

"I'm just going to have them check me and then we're going home." She says it calm but I can tell she's a little worried because even though she's breathing deep she's got her arms wrapped under her belly like she's trying to keep that baby in there.

Someone rolls in a wheelchair and Mom holds out a hand. "I'm fine." Tucker pushes it along next to her just in case and Mom keeps her other arm around my shoulders and I'm not sure who's holding who up.

The nurses in Labor and Delivery hand Mom a clipboard and Mom says, "I'm thirty-five weeks."

She kisses the top of my head and then she kisses Tucker's too and I'm wondering when she started kissing their heads like that but I'm not even mad about it because I'm glad he's there. A nurse tells Mom to sit in the wheelchair and Mom says, "I'll be right back. This will be nothing."

Cameron and Wendell and Bryce all get to the waiting room at the same time and Wendell is asking a hundred questions and the nurses are saying they're going to get as much information as they can.

And then Wendell sits down. No, he doesn't sit down, he collapses and falls down on a chair in the waiting room and he buries his head in his hands and cries. And I'll tell you one thing. I've seen Wendell cry before. Lots. That proud-happy-snort-cry. But I've never seen him cry like this. And it scares me. The nurse is trying to give him a cup of water and tell him that she's sure she'll have news on his wife soon. Cameron smiles at the nurse and takes the cup of water and I know what his smile is saying. It's saying that he's crying about more than that.

He's crying about the last time he rushed to a waiting room like this, eleven years ago, with baby Bryce in his arms and Cameron and Tucker clutching his sides. It was Mom's first day back to work after I was born and they were the first people she saw. Wendell and Cameron and Tucker and baby Bryce. Crying. All crying.

In the seats next to me, Cameron, Tucker, and Bryce slump over Wendell and they're a pile of arms and shoulders and hair and I'm trying to figure out if I should sit right next to their heap or skip a chair, when an arm reaches out, and I'm not even sure whose arm it is, but it's pulling me in and then I'm a part of the huddle too and I don't even really mind that I'm squished in tight to Bryce.

It feels like a hundred years until a doctor comes out and tells us Mom is doing great and we can see her. We follow her down the hall and into a room where Mom is lying in a bed. She has a bunch of wires connected to her belly and a monitor above her head that's ticking and beeping and feeding out a long piece of paper like a slow printer.

The doctor explains to us that Mom was having some contractions but she isn't actually in labor yet. She says some things I don't understand about the baby's heartbeat and lungs and Mom's blood pressure and how she may be at risk for preterm labor. "We want to keep that baby in there for as long as possible," she says.

Wendell is holding Mom's hand and Cameron and Tucker are on one side of the bed and Bryce and I are squeezed in on the other.

The doctor says she'll give Mom a shot that will help the baby's lungs develop a little quicker in case it comes early.

Then Wendell asks about Mom's heart. He clears his throat and says, "The boys' mom died here. Peripartum cardiomyopathy. Is . . . Is there a chance . . . have you . . ." There are tears on Wendell's face.

"Louise's heart is healthy," the doctor assures him.

Then she looks at all of us and says, "I don't blame the baby if it tries to come early." She smiles. "Babies know, even from the inside, what a great family they have waiting for them."

That gets Wendell snorting and squeezing Mom's hand and Mom doesn't even tell him to cut it out.

The doctor tells us they're going to keep Mom overnight and she can go home in the morning. "But no more high-action ambulance work." She looks right at my mom and says, "Desk work, Louise. No more work overnights. Slow walks. Easy stretches." And when Mom sighs, the doctor says, "For the baby."

I look back at the doctor and give her a nod like *even if my mom is an Embers, and it's hard for an Embers to be still, I got this.*

I lean down to hug Mom and she kisses me on the top of my head and says she loves me all the way up to the Care Bears, and that makes my eyes burn but before I let any tears leak out I bite my tongue in the back of my mouth and blink fast.

Wendell puts his arm around me and we all five walk out together and I'll tell you one thing. It doesn't actually feel so bad being all linked up with the Valentines right now. And I'm thinking about what that doctor said about the baby knowing its family and I'm wondering if the baby can really hear us already. So I make a little promise to myself that I'll try to say nicer things.

I call Grandma Bea on Tucker's cell phone on the way home and tell her about Mom. She asks a hundred questions and I try to answer them all but I didn't understand everything the doctor said except that Mom was going to be OK and she has to stop working overnight shifts. Only desk work. No more ambulance rides.

"Thank goodness," Grandma says.

I call Aunt Tam and tell her the same thing. I can tell she's worried because her voice shakes but she says OK and thanks for calling.

When we all get back to the house, Wendell takes three pizzas out of the freezer. They won't all fit in the oven at one time, so we cook two then slide another one in while we're eating those and I can tell we're all thinking about my mom, and maybe theirs, because it's pretty quiet, which it never is, until Cameron takes a long drink of water and says, "She'll be fine. The baby too."

"Yeah," says Bryce.

Wendell stretches his arms around us and we all kind of lean in over the counter and put our heads together. "I know," Wendell says. "We're all so lucky to have each other."

I'm crunched in right close to Bryce again, but I am feeling lucky. Lucky that Mom's OK and that she was there eleven years ago to hand Wendell cups of water, and boxes of raisins, and a warmed bottle of formula in the waiting room of the ER. And lucky that she ran into him a year later with Bryce and me in front-facing packs on their chests at the grocery store days after they had moved to our town. The story goes Bryce and I took one look at each other and started crying. So I guess I'm lucky too that over the years they became friends anyway. And then better friends. And now we're all here huddled around the counter with pizza.

Wendell's about to start snorting again when that awful doorbell starts to chime. I open the door when it's halfway through its song and Grandma Bea is standing there with a whole pound bag of M&M's. "I just missed you."

She comes in and hugs everyone and we move dinner from the counter to the table and Grandma Bea sits in Mom's seat and grabs a slice. She pushes the M&M's to the middle of the table and everyone says thanks for the dessert.

"Oh no no," Grandma Bea says. "I don't believe in that *dessert* hogwash. You have to eat your sweet with the rest because there's no time like the present." Then she reaches over and takes a handful of M&M's and tucks them beneath the layer of cheese on her pizza. She takes a big bite and smiles. "Like that," she says with a full mouth.

Then everyone, even Wendell, is tucking M&M's beneath their cheese and hollowing out the crust and restuffing it with their favorite colors and just as Bryce is reaching for another fistful, I hear a knock-knock-knockity-knock on the front door. Then another knock-knock-knockity-knock. And I'd know that knock anywhere. It's Aunt Tam's shared-wall goodnight knock. I jump up and knock-knock-knockity-knock back and then open the door and she's standing there with a thermos of hot chocolate. "I made too much," she says.

Cameron gets out seven mugs and fills each one halfway and Aunt Tam grabs a stool from the counter and squeezes in between Cameron and me.

Wendell says, "We don't need to tell Louise we had pizza, M&M's, and hot chocolate for dinner." We all laugh and sip and reach for more slices.

Then Cameron tells us that he talked with his teacher and they scheduled his two-day fake baby assignment for a time next month when he didn't have any college interviews, but that he'd have to take the baby to morning swim practice.

"Fake baby?" Grandma Bea asks.

Cameron fills her in on his Behavioral Science class and the crying doll and the wrist-locked key and Aunt Tam smiles and says, "It can't cry more than little Bea did."

"You can say that again," Grandma adds and smiles like she's remembering. "That's my girl. Never settle." And I know that means I never settled as a baby. That I clenched my fists and protested and used my voice at full volume. But I also know that Grandma's telling me to *Never settle*. Never settle for what doesn't feel right and fair. And I'll tell you one thing. Principal Meesley shrugging off our list and all our questions about soccer doesn't feel right and fair. And I'm not going to settle.

Grandma Bea leans across the corner of the table for a secret little Embers-girls fist bump then takes a few M&M's from the bag and drops them into her hot chocolate. Bryce is next to try it and then all our hands are grabbing extra M&M's and watching them sink to the bottom of our mugs where they melt into colorful clumps. We have to dig them out with a spoon and it's delicious. "Never tried that before!" Grandma Bea says, licking her spoon. "I like it."

Everyone's laughing and has melty chocolate mustaches and I'm thinking that I might like this new table and that I wish Mom were here because if the baby really can hear us from the inside, this would be a good moment to listen in on.

Aunt Tam hugs everyone before she leaves and she squeezes Wendell and Cameron and Tucker and Bryce just as long as she squeezes me and I'm thinking that's

OK. We're all worried about Mom and the baby and maybe just this once we're all starting to feel more like a team.

Grandma Bea stays and watches the Red Sox game with me and Wendell and Cameron and Tucker and Bryce and even though baseball is a hundred times slower than soccer, Tucker jumps up every time the count is full or there are two outs and he yells at the TV like we're right there in the stadium, and that makes it fun to watch. Grandma Bea joins him wildly cheering and they both burst into loud whoo-hoos and a full-on happy dance when we hit a home run.

Bryce and I are sitting on the floor in front of the couch, leaning against Cameron's and Wendell's legs, and Grandma Bea and Tucker nearly trip over us during their home run celebration. Bryce and I pull our knees to our chests and roll our eyes at them at the same time. That kind of gets us laughing and I'm thinking that Bryce's laugh isn't so bad when he's not being a bully-follower. And I wonder what Kenny and Morris would think if they could see Bryce around our big table, or taking care of Dodger and Roscoe and Fred, or right now, with all of us, laughing at his wildly dancing big brother and his not-grandma Bea.

He's a different person in these in-between times.

And I'm wondering if Kenny and Morris are too.

Grandma Bea tucks me in before she leaves and I

scooch over to give her a seat on the edge of my bed. I fill her in on Principal Meesley and Maximilian being our manager and the new girl, Cece. How she plays soccer and knows a whole language she can speak with her hands. And how Aileyanna and I are going to knock on Principal Meesley's door again.

"And again and again," Grandma says. "Give him hell . . . mann's mayonnaise."

I laugh and tell her I will and pretend to spread Hellmann's mayonnaise on a piece of bread. She smiles and pulls up Mom's old comforter.

"Three," she says. "Let's hear them."

"But it's not morning."

She waves her hand like that's not important. "Things won't always go exactly the same way forever," she tells me. "Now, give me three, even if it's eight hours early."

I smile and say, "One, that Mom and the baby are OK. Two, that Cece wants to play soccer. Three, M&M's in hot chocolate."

"Those are good ones," she whispers and kisses the top of my head.

12

HIS OFFICE IS LOCKED. We sit and wait in the lobby outside until the bell rings, then Aileyanna tells Ms. Landry that we'll be back.

She looks right at each of us and says, "Good." And the way she says it sounds like maybe what she really wants to say is *give him Hellmann's mayonnaise.*

"Tell him we were here," I say.

"Oh I will."

When we get to homeroom the American Sign Language alphabet and numbers one through ten are hanging big across the front wall. Ms. Kravitz tells us she put some sign language dictionaries in the back for us to use too if we want.

Ms. Blaise says we're going to do a quick check-in

on what we think of this school year so far. "Zero to ten. Zero is worst, ten is best." Then she points to the sign language numbers on the wall and raises her own hand and says, "But let's practice first. Then you can tell us with just one hand."

Cece is sitting with Maximilian and me and her interpreter is signing everything Ms. Blaise is saying.

Ms. Blaise starts counting. "Zero . . . one . . . two . . ." and moving her fingers in exactly the way I'd expect for counting, except she does *three* with her thumb. Then when she gets to *five* she stops and looks at all of us like she's telling us to really watch and then she touches her thumb to her pinkie and says, "Six."

Ms. Kravitz is circling around the room helping people with their hands and Cece and her interpreter, Ms. R, help Maximilian shake a little thumbs-up for *ten*. "Cool," he says.

"This *is* cool," Quinn says, and then Mac does too.

Ms. R keeps pointing to everyone who says *cool* then she presses her thumb to her chest, right below her shoulder and wags her fingers. *Cool*.

So then I look at Cece and try it out, wagging my own fingers. *Cool*, I tell her.

Then she presses her fingers to her lips and brings them forward toward me.

"Thank you," Ms. R says.

Cece and I both smile because when we look around everyone's pressing their thumbs to their chests and wagging their fingers.

After we practice counting with one hand, Ms. Blaise calls our attention and says, "So, from zero to ten, show me how much you're liking this school year so far."

I'm not sure what number to put up. Some parts are a ten. Like sitting with Maximilian and Cece and having Ms. Blaise and Ms. Kravitz. Some parts are a zero like Principal Meesley. I'm about to put up a seven when we hear the crackle of the loudspeaker and Principal Meesley's voice saying, "Aileyanna Absalon and Bea Embers, please report to my office."

Ms. R is pointing to the speaker in the corner of the ceiling and signing to Cece, and a few kids in the back are going *Oooooooh*, but Aileyanna and I stand up fast because this might be the only time it's a good thing to be called to the office.

Principal Meesley is on the phone when we get there so we have to sit outside and wait with Ms. Landry until he's done. It's only a few minutes but it feels like forever until we hear him say goodbye and hang up the big, clunky office phone. His door is still closed but I'm expecting him to open it any second.

When he doesn't, Ms. Landry nods at us and Aileyanna and I both give two hard knocks on his door, then turn the handle and go in.

"There you are," Principal Meesley says like we're the ones who have been hard to find.

"Here we are," I say.

He shuffles paper around on his desk then gestures for us to sit down at the little round table in his room. There are four chairs and I'm wondering if this is where you sit when you get sent to the office and they call your parents, and for one tiny second I'm thinking maybe we're actually in trouble.

We sit and Principal Meesley wheels his fancy chair around his desk and glides into the table right next to me. He's a hundred feet taller than we are in that chair so he has to kind of look down at us when he talks and I'm trying to look at his eyes like Mom taught me but from this angle I can see that he has little bunches of hairs tucked up in each nostril. I bite my tongue in the back of my mouth and try not to laugh.

There's a knock on the door and Emmie and Micah stick their heads in and Emmie says, "We heard you getting called to the office? Is this about the team?"

Meesley sighs and gestures that they can come in. So they do. He pulls out a calendar, takes a deep, grumbling breath and says, "OK. You can have your team."

We share quick, excited looks until he says *But*.

"But, we don't know how this will go, being the first

148

year and all. So, we're not hiring a coach."

There's another knock and it's Georgia. "Is it about the team?" she asks. I nod. Fern and Cece and Ms. R are behind her and they don't even ask to come in. They just do.

"He told us we can have a team but they're not hiring a coach," Micah fills them in.

"But we need a coach," Fern says.

"Now hang on a second. I'm going to be your coach."

"What?"

Cece watches Ms. R's hands and then she signs *No* with thumb, index, and middle fingers closing hard together like she's trying to shut off that idea.

"But you're the boys' coach . . ." Emmie starts.

The door to the office keeps opening. Cara, Jamie, Nelle. Then Tess and Quinn. Last is Maximilian and when he comes in there are thirteen of us and Principal Meesley doesn't look so big on his fancy chair anymore.

"I will have to coach both teams," he explains. "Boys will practice Mondays, Wednesdays, and Fridays. Girls on Tuesdays and Thursdays."

I look at Aileyanna because I can't really tell if this is good news or not. My heart is beating that fast *team-team team-team* but something deep in my gut is telling me that this might be some bullsharky.

"What do you mean you're not sure how this will

149

go?" Aileyanna asks. "You think we're going to quit?"

"I've been playing soccer my whole life," I say. "I'm not about to quit."

There is a loud echo of "Me too."

"I'm just saying." He holds up his hands like *don't shoot the messenger* except he isn't just the messenger, he's the whole message. "Many of you have quit before." He looks at Tess and Emmie and Micah and says, "We don't have the budget for another coach this year, and it would be a waste anyway if after the first game you decided that this isn't really what you imagined. Even if just one of you decides that . . ." He pushes the schedule over toward me. "Here. I entered you in the league. This is your game schedule."

His suit jacket kind of brushes my arm as he slides the schedule on the table and the wheels on his rolly chair bump into my foot and I'm thinking about what Grandma Bea says about elbow room. So I take a little.

I stick my elbows out wide and take up as much room as I can and it pushes back on his suit jacket a little.

I want to reach for the schedule but I still have that feeling deep down in my gut.

"How come the boys get three days?" I ask.

Principal Meesley huffs a sigh and says, "They have a nine-years-winning title to defend. Now they have to do it in three days a week. You've already taken two days from them, girls."

He says *girls* like this conversation is over. Then he stands up and says, "I'll see you on Field B on Tuesday. Make sure you have proper attire, cleats, and mouth guards."

"Why not Field A?" Nelle asks.

"Have to keep Field A in good condition for games," he says.

"But the boys are practicing there."

"Have a good weekend," he says. Then he kind of walks us out the door like we're a flock of sheep he's herding into the hallway.

Ms. Landry smiles and says, "Go, team!" and I want to smile and be excited too, but my gut still feels like this isn't good news. *Coach* Meesley?

Mom is back from the hospital when I get home. She's looking through Cameron and Tucker's "had to own it" shelves and pulling a couple of books out by their spines.

"Aren't those books for kids?" I ask her.

She gives me a big hug and the baby pushes into me too and I'm telling her to squeeze less because I'm kind of afraid she'll go into labor at any second.

"First, no," she says. "These books are for everyone.

And second, no. Nothing could ever make me squeeze you less."

I tell Mom she's supposed to be lying down as much as she can.

"That's not much," she jokes. But then she says, "OK, I know, I know. That's why I'm picking out some books." She lies down on the couch with Pete the Cat and a book called *Diary of a Wimpy Kid*. I sit down and put her feet over my lap and tell her all about Principal Meesley and the meeting and how we were all there and we have a team and a schedule but it still doesn't feel good. Not as good as it should.

"*He's* going to coach?"

I nod.

"And how come the boys get three days?"

"That's what I asked!" Then I tell Mom what he said, about how we took two days away from the boys' team already.

Mom is about to say *That's some bullsharky!* But before she can, I tell her to relax. For the baby.

And just as she's taking a deep breath we hear Wendell's car pull into the driveway and then the door to the garage flies open and Bryce comes in from soccer practice still wearing his shin guards and drops his backpack and stomps into the living room and says, "If we lose the championship, it'll be your fault. Guess you got what you wanted. Hope you're happy."

I'm about to tell him that if they lose the championship it'll be *his* fault, actually, because maybe they'll have a ref who calls offsides. And I'm about to tell him I didn't get what I wanted, actually. What I wanted was practice five days a week and a coach who doesn't think we're going to quit after the first game. But before I can say anything, Wendell gives me a little look and a *cut it out* gesture. Like he knows something I don't. Like I should drop it.

So I just say, "Whatever," which is something Grandma Bea tells me I should never say and Bryce runs upstairs and starts a shower.

"What was that about?" Mom asks.

"Coach told them at practice that they would have to knock down to three days a week so the girls could practice too," Wendell tells us.

"Oh no, I know that part." She sits up. "Bea, can you give us a minute?"

I roll my eyes and grab my backpack and head up to my room but really I stop and sit on the top step to listen.

I hear Mom whisper-yelling, "What I'm wondering is why you told Bea to cut it out. Bryce said something harsh to her then you shut her down."

"Louise, that's not what I meant."

"It doesn't matter what you meant. That's what you did."

There's murmuring that I can't hear and I can tell Wendell is trying to get Mom to sit down and relax.

Then Mom says, "And don't you for one second think about trying to explain that man's side, because that man just told a bunch of boys that it's the girls' fault they don't have practice every day. And that, Wendell, is some serious bullsharky."

I pump my fist because Mom's right and I wonder for a half second if maybe Mom will decide we don't need all these boys and we can pack up and go back to the condo. But I know better by now. They have little squabbles like this and then they think about it and talk and then everything's fine again. Maybe even better. And maybe I'm not so sure I don't want all the Valentines anymore because there's something deep down in my gut hoping I hear Mom and Wendell hug.

The shower turns off and I rush into my room before Bryce comes out in a towel, and I wish I could walk over to Maximilian's and not knock on the door. So we could run through the woods on our tramped-down path to the climbing tree.

I try the walkie-talkie but I already know it doesn't work.

So I pull out *Bridge to Terabithia* and read about

Jess's art and how his drawings help him calm down. And how his dad gets angry because he doesn't want his *only son* to turn into some artist. That gets me so mad. I even have to shut the book for a minute because no one should tell someone they can't do something just because they're a girl or a boy or whatever. I know exactly what Grandma Bea would say about that. *It's some hogwash.* That's what she'd say. And she'd be right.

13

PRINCIPAL MEESLEY DROPS A worn cardboard box on the sideline of Field B. "Welcome to your first practice." I can tell the tape on the box has been peeled off and retaped a hundred times because the sticky part is fuzzy with bits of cardboard and the whole strip is flapping in the breeze.

He tells us to line up, that we're getting our uniforms. He hands Maximilian a notebook and pencil and says, "Write down what I say."

We all stand in front of the bench and Principal Meesley reaches his hand in the box and pulls out a pile of unfolded school uniforms, white with green numbers. He shakes out a jersey and tosses it to Quinn.

He points at her. "Quinn?" he says, like he hasn't

been her principal since kindergarten.

Quinn nods.

"Number twenty-one. Quinn," Meesley says. Maximilian writes it down.

He points to Emmie and peels another uniform off the pile. "Emmie. Number six." Maximilian writes.

I shift my feet a little and try to see the numbers on the jerseys bunched in his hand. I shoot a glance to Aileyanna and I know we're both thinking this isn't how it's supposed to go. We're supposed to tell Principal Meesley what positions we play, have a couple of practices, and prove that we should be number ten. It's not supposed to be just random like this. Like our numbers don't even matter.

Georgia gets twelve. Tess gets four. Micah is sixteen.

Then Principal Meesley gets to Cece. Ms. R doesn't come to soccer practices because she works for the school and her day ends at three o'clock, but Cece signed that she didn't care, she would play anyway.

"Cecelia," he says. I think she can see her long name on his lips because she curves her hand in the letter *C*.

"Cece," we tell him. "Her name is Cece."

"OK. *Cece* then." He tosses her the next jersey. "Number ten."

Aileyanna and I both say, "But Principal Meesley!" at the same time.

"That's my number," I tell him. "I've always been number ten."

"Me too," Aileyanna says.

He tells us to relax, and that our numbers don't matter, like we don't know that number ten controls the field, that number ten is the playmaker, that number ten should be double-teamed, triple-teamed. That number ten is a not-so-secret weapon.

"Got that, Maximilian?"

He nods and writes it down and gives me a look like he's sorry.

I shake my head and Principal Meesley tosses me number one and I look at him like he better not be thinking for one second I'm going to be in goal. Number one is a goalie's number and I'll tell you one thing. That's not me.

Aileyanna gets nine. Striker. Goal scorer. Brilliant finisher. Making flashy runs into the penalty box and one-touching into the corners then pulling your shirt over your face and celebrating as the team lifts you up because you scored the game winner in the last minute.

She smiles at me but I whisper back, "He says our numbers don't matter, remember?" And she looks at me like *you know they do.*

Principal Meesley assigns the rest of the numbers and tells us to pull our jerseys on over our shirts. I don't

158

know how to sign that to Cece, but she's looking at Fern and Nelle pulling on their uniform tops so she follows and pulls number ten over her head.

"These don't smell washed," Cara says.

"That's because they're not," he answers.

"Ewww."

Georgia looks at Cece and plugs her nose and makes a gross face and pretends she's trying to wave the stink out of her jersey. Cece laughs and plugs her nose too.

"If you can't handle sweat, you can call it quits right now. Just let me know." I almost say I don't see him wearing other people's old sweat, but I bite my tongue in the back of my mouth, and he tells us we're going to start with a little running.

"Two laps." He blows the whistle around his neck and we all take off around the field.

Emmie starts out in front and Aileyanna and I are right behind her. We're all running together because this is a warm-up, but when we round our lap we hear Principal Meesley say, "Number six. Fast start." Maximilian writes it down.

Our second lap doesn't feel like a warm-up anymore. It feels like a race. Emmie is still out front, but I'm gaining on her and Aileyanna is right on my heels. As soon as Cece sees us all picking up the pace she does too and zooms to the front of the pack and is neck and neck with

Emmie. I look back and see Georgia and Fern trailing and Nelle is last, almost half a field behind us.

We cross by Principal Meesley and collapse, breathing hard, and I hear him say something about number one and number nine and number ten but my heart is beating too hard in my ears so I can't make out what he says. Maximilian keeps writing.

We wait for Nelle and clap when she crosses but Principal Meesley hollers, "You're the last one, number thirteen! You got to do better than that." At first I'm mad he called her out like that, but then I'm also relieved I wasn't the last one and I hate that I have that feeling. Then he says something under his breath to Maximilian.

"What did you say?" I ask.

"I'm just making notes," Principal Meesley says. "For myself. Figuring out what positions everyone can play, who has skills . . ." he says.

I look at Maximilian, but he keeps his eyes on the paper.

Aileyanna cuts in, "I can tell you what position I play. I've played midfield for . . ."

"Got it," he says, then blows his whistle. And the way he's acting makes me wonder if he's trying to get one of us to quit so he can say I told you so, and that we don't have enough players for a team, and then he can go back to coaching the boys five days a week.

I put my arm around Nelle's shoulders and tell her she did great and that first days always stink. She's breathing hard and trying not to cry, but it doesn't work. Tears start falling down her cheeks and landing on her wrinkly uniform.

I glare at Principal Meesley and I see him lean toward Maximilian and say something else. Maximilian hesitates and shakes his head and taps the eraser of his pencil four times on the notebook page.

Principal Meesley chuckles and nudges him. "You can go ahead and write *sensitive* next to your name then," he says, and snickers again like he's so funny, but Maximilian isn't laughing. Then Meesley points to the notebook and gives him a look like *write* and leans in toward him again. But I know Maximilian. He won't write anything mean about anybody because he's not mean. He's my best friend.

Cece taps me on the shoulder and is holding her arms out like she wants to know what's going on and I wish I knew the signs for *Principal Meesley is the worst ever,* but instead I point to Nelle's tears and then to Meesley and it looks like Cece can read my face and read Nelle's tears and Principal Meesley's body language because she puts her arm around Nelle too.

Next we practice dribbling and Principal Meesley's

blowing his whistle for us to dribble and stop and dribble and change directions and dribble again. Cece dribbles with her head up, watching Principal Meesley's whistle, then watching what we do. She has good control of the ball the whole time because she almost never needs to look down.

Aileyanna has quick ball-handling skills, dribbling around the cones in the eighteen-yard box.

I do a couple of moves. A step-over-scissor around a make-believe defender, then I dribble right up to Meesley and fake right and go left around him so he can see how much control I have over the ball. So he'll put me in midfield.

Principal Meesley is still calling out numbers and notes to Maximilian and even though Meesley is the worst ever creeping water bug I still want a hundred good notes next to my number. Notes like *fast* and *strong left foot*.

Cara loses her ball outside of the box and hustles off to get it before Principal Meesley notices. Then Tess and Emmie crash into each other and instead of laughing and collecting their balls and dribbling on, they look at Meesley, hoping he didn't see, then they yell at each other.

"Watch where you're going!" Tess says.

"What's your problem?"

Principal Meesley sees them and whispers something to Maximilian. Maximilian shakes his head and I can hear Meesley telling him about how sports isn't all rainbows and unicorns and the girls have to get used to that. "Am I right?" he says and gives him another little nudge.

I want to tell him that Maximilian doesn't like jokey little nudges but I just keep dribbling. I slow down and bring the ball close to the sideline so I can try to hear more but Meesley just calls us in and says the last thing we'll do today is shots on goal.

He tells Maximilian to get in goal.

"I don't play, Principal Meesley. Just numbers for me."

But Meesley isn't listening and tosses Maximilian a pair of goalie gloves. "Well, you're in goal today."

I can see him starting to shake his head and breathe heavy and Meesley isn't doing a thing about it and everyone on the team is looking around and down like *No way do I want to play goalie* so I stop rolling the ball beneath my left cleat and run to him. "It's OK, Maximilian. I'll be in goal." I take the gloves and sneak a squeeze in the web between his thumb and forefinger and whisper, "Eight, sixteen, twenty-four."

He takes a breath and whispers "thirty-two" and slides the notebook on the bench and sits down next to it. I put on the old, crusty goalie gloves. They're too big so I pull the Velcro tight on my wrists and give them a clap. Little bits of the padding from the palms crumble off.

Meesley mumbles something about how he's being nice even counting Maximilian as a manager. Then he calls, "A! You're up first."

Aileyanna pops her orange mouth guard back in and sets the ball up on the penalty kick line. She takes three big steps back and glares straight into the left corner of the net, but I bet she's trying to fake me out and she's really going right, so just as she's about to strike the ball I dive right and feel the ball smack against my gloves. It clears the post.

"What a save!" Emmie calls.

I don't want to be good at goalie, though, because I want to play midfield. But I also don't want to look bad and get cruddy notes next to my name, and I'm not one for not trying my best so I take a few hops and get ready for the next shot.

Aileyanna jogs off, shaking her head, and Cece's next.

She smiles at me with her bright blue mouth guard and waves her crossed fingers back and forth. I remember from Ms. Blaise's classroom wall that crossed fingers like that is an *R* in the ASL alphabet. Cece signs it again and her face is asking a question. *Ready?*

I nod and she backs up four little steps. She doesn't

strike it as hard as Aileyanna so I see it sailing to the upper left corner. I jump and punch it up over the goal.

Meesley claps and nods his head. "Atta girl!" And I hate that that feels pretty good.

I save Micah's. Georgia misses wide. Nelle scores in the upper right corner. Jamie sends it sailing over the top of the goal and Fern's shot barely makes it to me so I scoop it up easily.

At the end of practice Principal Meesley hands out copies of our schedule and says he'll see us Thursday. Aileyanna is following him as he picks up the cones and she's saying, "I've played midfield since second grade and I can strike with both feet . . ." But he just turns and tells Maximilian to collect the balls. Aileyanna continues, "And I can flip throw-in."

"I can too!" I call.

Meesley nods and grabs the last cone off the field. "And please remind your parents I have a don't-talk-to-me-during-the-games policy. They can find me another time if they want to." I think of his locked door, *Do Not Disturb*, and think, yeah right.

We all pass the balls slowly over to Maximilian and he shoos them in the bag then cinches the top and hands it to Principal Meesley.

Maximilian whispers "thank you" to me and I put my hands on his shoulders. Wendell honks from the parking lot and Maximilian waves to him then walks across the field to our path back to the condos.

I pull off my jersey number one and when Principal Meesley turns his back and all the girls are unlacing their cleats and pulling on their sweatshirts, I see his notebook on the bench. Maximilian is supposed to keep track of that so I quickly slide it into my backpack with my stinky uniform and start jogging toward Wendell's car.

"Hey there, soccer star!" Wendell says. "I didn't know you could play in goal too."

"Yeah," I answer. "But that was just today. We don't have a goalie yet."

"You were amazing." Wendell starts the car. "And Coach Meesley knows the old rule; if you don't have a keeper, put your best athlete back there because they'll pick it up the quickest."

"Principal Meesley doesn't know anything," I tell him. "He was pushing Maximilian to be in goal which, if you know Maximilian for one second, you know that soccer balls flying at his face is not a good idea. That's why I was in goal. Not because Meesley knows anything."

"I see," Wendell says. "Well, I'm glad you got a chance to show your stuff." It's silent for a moment then he taps his fingers on the wheel and says, "I'm sorry I cut you off last night. Bryce was out of line. So was Coach Meesley."

"Thanks," I say. Then it's silent for a little longer and I'm thinking about how it sounds weird to hear Wendell call him *Coach* Meesley. Because I'll tell you one thing. I'm not calling him *Coach*. No way.

"Well," Wendell says, "he has to know *something* if he's got such a winning record. Nine straight seasons." And I know he's trying to make me feel better but I don't want to feel better yet. I just want to be mad for a minute and have Wendell be quiet.

"He doesn't want our team to win. He wants us to quit, actually."

"Bea, that's not true."

He pulls the car in the driveway and I look him straight in the eyes to make sure he's listening. "It is true."

He squinches his eyebrows together and puts his hand on my shoulder. Then he says he has to go get Tucker at band practice and he'll be right back.

Bryce and Mom are at the kitchen stools and Bryce is showing her Ms. Kravitz's iPad. "So I can listen to the book while I follow along." He plugs in the earbuds and holds one to my mom's ear.

"This is the coolest," she says. "I wish I had this when I was in school."

I drop my bag on the floor and Mom looks up and pulls the earbud out. "Bea! How was it?" She comes over and kisses me on the head.

"Shouldn't you be sitting or lying or getting your pelvis up, whatever that means?"

Mom laughs and says, "After a day of desk work, standing feels great." But I point to the couch and she says, "OK, OK" and lies down with a pillow beneath her hips. Bryce puts both earbuds in his ears and keeps reading.

"So?" she asks.

"It was pretty terrible. Principal Meesley almost made Maximilian spin out of control. And he didn't even care what numbers we wanted. Then I ended up playing goalie, and I was pretty good so I'll probably be stuck there all season."

Mom is shaking her head and asking about Maximilian and she's not lying down anymore and the pillow from her hips has slipped.

"Mom," I say, and I point for her to lie back down. "Pelvis."

She takes a deep breath and lies back down and I bite my tongue in the back of my mouth and say, "It's OK. Don't worry about Meesley. I got this."

Mom says OK but to keep her in the loop, and that she's going to head out for a little walk before it gets too dark. "The doctor said that was OK, remember?" I tell her to take it easy and she promises.

Then I grab my bag and I'm heading upstairs to take a shower when Bryce pulls his earbuds out. "What number did you get?"

I sign *one* to him and he laughs. "Keeper?"

"No," I say. "He just assigned them randomly."

"Randomly? That's not what he did for us."

There's a fire in my gut.

"Who got number ten?" he asks.

"Cece," I say.

And even though I don't ask him he says, "I'm ten. We just have to wait for our new uniforms to get here later this week."

"New uniforms?"

"Yeah," he says. "They're coming right before our first game." Then he puts his earbuds in and goes back to reading.

I run up the stairs and slam my door and press my face into my pillow and scream through the cotton case and into the squishy filling where my scream gets trapped. I scream and scream because Bryce is number ten and their numbers matter, and I scream and scream because those stinky uniforms Meesley tossed at us during practice were the boys' old hand-me-downs.

When I stop screaming I can hear Wendell's and

Tucker's muffled voices outside talking to someone and I'm wondering if it's Aileyanna but I don't want to go downstairs so I tiptoe into Bryce's room so I can look out his window to the front yard.

His shin guards are hanging from the knob on his closet door and his floor is covered with clothes. I step over a pair of dirty soccer socks and crumpled jeans and I kind of have to lean over his desk to see all the way out the window and when I do I knock a stack of notebooks off his desk. I'm hoping he still has his earbuds in downstairs because I'm imagining him running up and catching me in his room and complaining to Wendell and then no one will ever believe me that Bryce ever does anything wrong.

I quickly pick up the notebooks and stick them back on his desk and I'm pretty sure he won't notice a thing because his desk is as messy as his floor. Except a picture falls from one of the notebooks and lands faceup on a pair of shorts on his floor. And as I'm trying to pick up the picture by the very corner so my fingers don't touch his clothes, I see that the picture is of the Valentines. All of the Valentines. It's one of those professional photos where they're all wearing the same thing, jeans and white shirts, and they're sitting out in front of the garden at their old house. Their mom is in the middle holding Bryce, who is sleeping and wearing a white onesie. Wendell sits behind them, with his arms around her, and he's looking down at the baby and Cameron and Tucker are smiling right at the camera. They are both missing front teeth.

The picture makes me sad, like I'm looking in on a big in-between time that only the Valentines should ever see, but I can't stop looking at it. How they're all matching. Like a team.

Then I hear the voices outside again and I quickly stuff the picture back in a notebook and look outside. There's a new car in Aileyanna's driveway and Wendell and Tucker are talking with a man who's wearing black pants and a long jacket. They shake hands with him and say a few more things then make their way toward the house and I wonder if that's Aileyanna's dad.

I hustle out of Bryce's room and back to my own, then unzip my backpack. Principal Meesley's notebook is shoved in with my stinky, wrinkly, hand-me-down number one jersey. I open it to the page from today's practice. On one side our names are jotted by our numbers, on the other are the notes about us, all in Maximilian's handwriting.

#21 Quinn: no first touch
#6 Emmie: fast start, no stamina
#12 Georgia: agreeable, could play anywhere

#4 Tess: clumsy

#16 Micah: weak shot

#10 Cece: surprisingly quick, hard to coach?

#13 Nelle: out of shape, sensitive

#9 A: skills, ego

#8 Fern: no power

#15 Cara: no control

#18 Jamie: slow

#1 Bea: goalie, attitude

I rip the page right out of the notebook and crumple it and throw it across my room straight at the share-with-Bryce wall and grab the pillow that still has my scream from earlier trapped in it and I scream again. I scream because Principal Meesley is turning Maximilian into a clinging molecule and I scream because Principal Meesley is the creepiest creeping water bug that ever existed.

I scream until I'm out of breath. Then I bite my tongue in the back of my mouth and I think: we're going to sink him.

14

I SIT DOWN HARD next to Maximilian and slide the crumpled piece of notebook paper across the table to him. He looks down at the list of notes and then down at his hands and shakes his head. Then he punches *Sorry* into his TI-84 and slides it toward me.

I push it back.

Then he takes the crumpled paper and jots something with his pencil at the bottom of the list.

Maximilian: weak

I pick up his TI-84 and write. *No more weak. No more notes. You're on our team.*

He nods and whispers, "Promise."

Ms. Blaise tells us to turn and talk to our partners about what we're reading and if we think it's a good book for us. Instead, I tell Maximilian and Cece about my plan for our team. Ms. R is signing everything I'm saying and I'm wondering if she's supposed to be telling us to get back on task because she's a grown-up. But she's also Cece's voice, and Cece is signing quickly about how to spread the word to the whole team that even though today is Wednesday, a boys' team day, we have practice.

Most of them have cell phones so they just sneak a text to their families to arrange rides and send me a thumbs-up.

I lean over to Aileyanna's table and whisper, "Was that your dad last night?"

She looks down at the cell phone in her hands beneath the table and whispers back, "Yeah, but he's already on his way back to Brooklyn."

I ask Ms. Kravitz if I can go to the bathroom but really I walk to the office to call home and tell Mom our plan. She says that's great and that Wendell will be there to pick up Bryce anyway so I can come home with him.

On my way back I poke my head into another classroom and say, "Sorry to interrupt, but I have a message for Emmie." Their teacher nods and Emmie hustles out to the hall. I tell her the plan and she pumps her fist *yes* and says she'll spread the word and we'll all meet at three o'clock on Field B. Then I do the same thing for the next classroom, giving the message to Micah, before I go back to Ms. Blaise and Ms. Kravitz's room.

It's silent when I get back to my table because every-one is reading. Bryce is scrolling on the iPad with his earbuds in and I can see Kenny and Morris making stupid little gestures behind him and Morris whispers, "That doesn't count as reading."

Kenny whispers back, "Right?"

And I don't know if I'm still just so mad about the notebook and Meesley, or if I'm picturing baby Bryce in his mom's arms in the Valentines' picture, or his purple glitter toothbrush propped in the cup in our bathroom, but before I sit down to read *Bridge to Terabithia* I walk back to their table and say. "Quit making fun of people."

Bryce pulls the earbuds from his ears when he sees me. "What?" he asks.

"Nothing," I tell him. "Your *friends* were just com-menting on your iPad, which is actually really cool, but they seem to think is funny."

Bryce throws them a look like *What the heck?* And Kenny mumbles, "Whatever," and I go back to my table.

Most people have stopped reading and are looking over the tops of their books at what's going on and Ms. Kravitz comes over and says, "That took strength, Bea. Thank you for reminding Kenny and Morris about kindness."

Then she sits with Bryce and says, loud enough for all of us to hear, "The iPad *is* cool, Bryce. And so is the special set of manipulatives Morris uses for math and so are the graphic organizers Kenny uses to help him take notes in social studies. Ms. R is cool because she helps us understand Cece's language. And counting by eights to calm down and rest your brain is cool too. Anyone who can figure out what helps them learn is cool in my book." Ms. Kravitz does the chest-point-waggly-fingers sign for *cool* and Bryce does it back.

And I'm thinking that Ms. Blaise and Ms. Kravitz are kind of like Grandma. Good captains. Because right now we all feel like a team and I know if I looked in their notebooks all the comments would be about how cool we are.

The class settles back into reading and in my book Jess has met the new girl on his road, Leslie, and it turns out she's the fastest kid in the fifth grade. Not Jess. And I'm thinking that they're going to be enemies, and for a few pages, Jess really *is* annoyed by her, how she dresses weird and how she ruined the running races by winning, and how she lives right there next to him, but then one day in his favorite teacher's class they're all singing this song and then Jess just decides to change his mind about her. And then they're friends. Best friends, like Maximilian and me. And they build a whole secret land out in the woods that sounds a whole lot like the stamped-down path and climbing tree behind the condos.

And I'm thinking that if Jess can just change his

mind about Leslie maybe I can just change my mind about Aileyanna, even if she's number nine and I'm number one, even if she wears fancy city clothes and moved here for a *quieter, slower* life, and maybe I can even just change my mind about Bryce too.

After school all thirteen of us gather in the hallway and I show them Principal Meesley's notes and everyone gasps and says *That's messed up* and *He doesn't know anything* and we're all getting mad, the kind of mad that makes you want to knock on doors and run faster and play harder. None of us has our smelly uniforms or even shorts or cleats, and we only have a few soccer balls between us, but it's not going to stop us from practicing. Our first game is next week and we won't be ready after one more practice with Meesley.

I fold the paper and slide it back between the pages of Principal Meesley's notebook, then put it back in my bag. We walk in a group out to Field B, next to where the boys' team is gathering on Field A. We huddle up and I say, "Let's get warm. Two laps." And before we start I add, "Together. Two laps together."

And we take off, even Maximilian, rounding the first corner, the sound of twenty-six feet padding along the grass, and our breath puffing into the air. After the second lap we see Principal Meesley and he's blowing his

177

whistle and waving us off the field. "Girls! It's Wednesday! Boys' day."

We run right by him because we said two laps. Two laps together. And that's what we're going to do because Principal Meesley is wrong. It's a girls' day.

He's waiting for us when we finish. "This isn't allowed," he says. "You cannot be here without supervision."

"You're here," Aileyanna says.

We start to circle up on the field for some stretches. Micah and Cece are leading in the middle but Principal Meesley says, "I'm not supervising you. I'm supervising the boys' team. This behavior will result in the cancellation of your team."

I look at Cece and I point to Meesley, then to my mouth, and then I do that fingers-closing sign. *He says no.* She nods then swoops her finger around the circle to point at all of us, then to her mouth, and wags a solid, powerful fist up and down. *We say yes.*

Principal Meesley tells us he doesn't have time for this and it's up to us, but if we choose to be out here unsupervised he'll pull our team from the league. "Which would be a lot easier for me, girls. But do as you please." He turns back to the boys on Field A.

We all look at each other and drop our shoulders and decide it's not worth being pulled from the league, so we'll have to come up with another plan. We pick up our things and sigh and huff and we're all saying *This is so unfair*. Then we walk together back toward the parking lot where we see Ms. Blaise and Ms. Kravitz shuffling to their cars holding tall stacks of our notebooks from English class. Inside one of those stacks is my notebook where I responded to Ms. Blaise's question *What are you reading and what is it making you think?* I wrote a few sentences about how Jess and Leslie are making me think that you should ignore what other people believe and do what you know is right and good. Like how Jess becomes friends with Leslie even though kids kind of make fun of her. But I'm also a little worried that Jess might not be that nice sometimes too because he made fun of a girl on the bus because she's big. And even though the girl is a bully, it still felt pretty cruddy when I read it.

And that makes me think that maybe even really good people, like Jess, and maybe even Wendell and Maximilian, can be clingy little molecules sometimes.

Ms. Blaise and Ms. Kravitz shift their stack of notebooks so they can wave. "What are you all doing?"

We run to them and explain about how we need more practice and how Principal Meesley is threatening to end our team because we need a supervisor but there's no chance we'll be ready for our first game and how he thinks we're going to lose anyway and we don't want to prove him right.

They look at each other. "There's a bench over there, right?" Ms. Kravitz asks.

We all nod.

"Guess reading these by the field is as good a place as any," she says. Ms. Blaise smiles and agrees and we all scream and jump and Georgia is pointing to our teachers and then to her eyes and out to the field. *They're going to watch us.* And Cece grabs Georgia's hands and jumps up and down with us too.

Ms. Blaise and Ms. Kravitz sit on the bench with the stacks of notebooks between them and they each take one from the top of the pile. They're reading and writing comments and smiling and nodding while we gather on the field to talk about positions.

Principal Meesley comes over and asks what's going on. Ms. Blaise looks up and says, "We're supervising." Then she looks back down at the notebook.

He shakes his head and walks back to the boys' field.

I take out Meesley's notebook and turn to a fresh page to draw the field.

"Does anyone want to play goalie?" Micah asks.

No one raises their hand but a few look at me. I shake my head and say, "Not really. I like midfield."

"We can take turns in goal," Aileyanna says, and the whole team agrees.

Everyone circles around as I draw the positions in

the notebook. "We'll have A, Bea, and Cece in the midfield," I say. Everyone laughs and A looks at me and smiles because I think maybe she notices that's the first time I called her *A*.

Cara, Jamie, and Micah all want to play forward.

Nelle jumps up and says, "Sweeper for me! That's what I played last year." Georgia wants to give stopper a try and Quinn and Emmie will team up as defensive backs.

Fern says she doesn't mind starting in goal for a bit and Tess says she's happy to be the first sub.

After I have all the positions jotted down I draw some arrows to show how we'll move up and down the field as a team. "Let's line up like this," A says, pointing to the notebook, "and just pass a ball around so we can get used to where we are."

We all run to our positions. A and I get to the center of the midfield at the same time. "I can take left," she says.

"We can switch. Keep the defenders on their toes."

She nods.

We pass the ball around the field. From me to Cece, and Cece up to Micah, over to Jamie, back to A, back to Quinn, and Nelle, and all the way to Fern in goal.

"Let's do it again!" I call. "This time, no flat passes. Only diagonals. Like this." I pass back to Emmie and she passes up to A.

When Cece calls for the ball she claps her hands. When we want Cece to make a run, we point to the spot on the field where we're going to put the ball. Then we start doing that for everyone. And before I know it, we're moving and talking like a team. Run, clap-clap, receive the ball, point, send it. We even shoot a few on Fern in goal and then we rotate Tess in for Quinn and she clap-claps and makes a run, one-touching it to A up the line.

After practice Maximilian calls us all in and shows us the notes he's been taking.

Number of passes: 88
Goals scored: 5
Goals saved: 2
Number of subs: 4

We read our team stats for the day and high-five and Tess says, "I can't believe you counted every pass!"

Maximilian smiles and Ms. Blaise calls over, "I can believe it! That kid's brain is wired for numbers. He's perfect for manager."

"I agree," I say and put my hands on the sides of his shoulders.

They stack their notebooks back up and call, "Good practice, girls!" as they make their way to their cars in the lot.

On Field A they're finishing up a drill where Principal Meesley feeds the ball and two boys take off as fast as they can to win the ball. "Be first!" he calls. Then he feeds another. Bryce and Morris take off and Bryce wins it by a mile but Morris complains that Bryce got a head start and Bryce whines back *did not!*

Principal Meesley waves them off and sends the next ball out across the field. Wyatt and Kenny take off and Kenny gets there first with enough time to get a touch on the ball but Wyatt is coming in fast and Kenny backs off and then Wyatt backs off too and they both end up just kind of standing there with the ball untouched between them.

They're about to laugh about it when Principal Meesley blows his whistle. "Scaredy-cats!" he hollers. "If you want to win games, you can't shy off the ball like a couple of little girls!"

Their whole team laughs. But ours doesn't.

Maximilian writes down what Meesley said in the notebook so Cece can read it and we're all shaking our heads and saying *Are you kidding?*

"What did you just say about girls?" I call. But he doesn't hear me because he's clapping his hands and sending out the next ball and hollering to the boys to *get to it!* like it was no big deal what he said, like I should just forget about it.

But I'll tell you one thing. I won't forget it.

Principal Meesley's whistle signals the end of the boys' practice and Wendell's pulling into the parking lot. But before we go, Cece claps her hands like she's calling for the ball and we all turn.

She puts her hand out and gestures to all of us to do the same. Emmie puts her hand in the middle, on top of Cece's, then Nelle and Fern and Cara and Jamie do too. All our hands, even Maximilian's, are blended together. We're watching Cece for what's next and she pulls her hand out from beneath and signs *One, two, three* then the sign we saw Ms. R do for *team*. Both *T* fists press together then move out and around until they meet again, closing the circle. Just like a *team*.

Cece puts her hand back in and we bounce *one, two, three* and pull out our fists to sign *team* all together. Then we watch Cece shake her open hands in the air like a roaring applause and one by one we do too. It's a silent, thunderous applause that gains momentum as each one of us adds in. Like we're cheering for ourselves and for each other and for the whole team.

And I'll tell you one thing. That was the best practice I've ever had. And when I get home I call Grandma Bea and ask her what she's doing Friday.

15

IN CLASS THE NEXT day Ms. Blaise is talking about making arguments. "We'll be practicing making claims and working to support them with evidence," she says.

I'm thinking I have a lot of points I want to argue to Principal Meesley. But it doesn't matter how much evidence our team has on any of our points, about why we deserve new uniforms too, or as many practice days as the boys, or a say in our jersey numbers or positions, if he's not listening. And he's not listening.

Ms. Kravitz joins in to say, "You can gather evidence in lots of different ways. For example, if I'm trying to argue that my dog is energetic, I might use my senses to prove it and jot down some things I see, or things I hear." She points to her eyes then her ears. "For example, I might jot down that he nudges me awake at five o'clock every morning. Or that he wags his tail so hard it knocks over everything on the coffee table." Everyone laughs.

She draws a chart in her notebook and we all know to copy it down in ours.

"Let's practice with someone in your own life. Under name, jot down a family member or a friend, or anyone you know."

I jot down *Grandma Bea.*

"Now think of a word that describes that person. A trait."

Positive.

"Now write one way you know that. Think of things you see them do or hear them say."

Grandma Bea's threes, I write.

Ms. Blaise is walking around and helping some kids with their charts and Ms. Kravitz is having a conference with Maddie's table to help them brainstorm some describing words. I'm done, so I add more people to my page.

Name	Trait	Evidence
Grandma Bea	Positive	-Grandma Bea's threes
Mom	Strong	-Ambulance driver -Stands up for me -Can do tons of push-ups
Aunt Tam	Loyal	-Walked with Mom when I cried all night -Friends forever

I almost add that Bryce is *annoying* and A is *show-offy*, but I don't, even though I have evidence to prove it, because I'm trying to be more like Jess from my book, and I'm starting to realize there is maybe more to them than just that.

Then as I'm writing, an idea comes flashing into my head so I wave for Maximilian's TI-84 and punch in a new part to our plan.

Keep writing Meesley's notes.

He reads it and raises his eyebrows like *What?* I punch more into the calculator and slide it back to him. He smiles and gives me a big thumbs-up. He even lets me pass his calculator around to Cece and Quinn and A and Georgia and Tess and Fern. I watch them as they read the screen and then look up to catch my eye and smile.

At the end of class Ms. Blaise checks in on my notebook. "That's quite a lineup," she says. "You're lucky."

I nod, and as she moves on to Maximilian's notebook I jot down my own name on the page, *Bea*. And then *Lucky*. And all my evidence is already there. Grandma Bea, Mom, Aunt Tam.

I bring Principal Meesley's notebook to recess and tear out the diagram of the field I drew yesterday at practice with all our positions on it. Then I give the notebook to

Maximilian and the crumpled piece of paper with his horrible notes jotted next to our names and jersey numbers.

"Copy them back in," I tell him.

Maximilian nods and sits against the bricks of the school, getting straight to work, and I find Emmie and Micah and Nelle, who say they'll spread the word to the rest of the team.

At the end of recess, Maximilian keeps Meesley's notebook, but hands me back the original wrinkly page with the mean comments. I crumple it again, into the tiniest ball I can, and stuff it deep down in my backpack.

When I get my reading notebook back at the end of the day I see Ms. Blaise's handwriting and I smile before I even read it because I know she wrote it from the bench supervising our soccer practice.

> Bea—I'm so glad you're enjoying _Bridge to Terabithia_. This is some smart thinking, and I believe you're right. People aren't ever just one thing. Not even main characters who we love. Not even bullies. People are complicated and usually worth taking the time to get to know. Keep it up.
> —Ms. Blaise

I'm trying to remember this at practice after school, but I'm pretty sure Principal Meesley _is_ just one thing.

Or maybe he is more complicated because he's mean *and* grumpy *and* a bad listener.

But I'll tell you one thing. I don't think he's worth taking the time to get to know because instead of looking at the diagram I'm showing him from yesterday or listening to us about our positions and how we practiced moving like a team, he's holding up a white board and drawing little *X*'s and saying we're going to run a six-three-one with the three midfielders playing defensively. A and I scoff and say *Are you kidding?* because what that means is six defenders, three midfielders, and one lone striker. What that means is he doesn't have confidence we'll score any goals so he's just stacking us back in front of our own goal.

"Before you start getting fancy with offense, let's see if between the eleven of you on the field you can manage to keep the ball from going in your own net."

I look at Maximilian. He writes that down and I give him a nod like he's got this.

Principal Meesley is asking for his notes from Tuesday and Maximilian turns back to the first page in the notebook, the one he rewrote during recess time.

Meesley starts calling out the numbers on our wrinkled, oversized jerseys and pointing to spots on the field. Even though my number one has been through the wash it still smells like decades of boys.

"How come the boys are getting new uniforms?" I ask.

He pulls the whistle around his neck and answers, "Two teams. Two sets of jerseys."

"But how come we got the old ones?" Tess asks.

"You just got a new team. Now you want new jerseys?" He shakes his head. "You can always fundraise. I'm happy to give you the name of the place we order from."

"Did the boys fundraise for theirs?" A asks.

But he just blows his whistle. "Number twenty-one," he calls, then points to the middle circle. "Striker."

I try to tell him that number twenty-one has a name and it's Quinn and she's actually a defensive back, but he's already pointing and shouting, "Number twelve! Number ten! Sweepers! We're running two sweepers."

"Number ten is Cece," A tells him. "You have to explain that to her."

Meesley looks at Cece and I can tell he doesn't have one idea about how to talk to her. "Tell her it's the last defender before the goalie and not to let anyone by," he says.

Maximilian sneaks a couple of quick jots in the notebook.

Georgia looks at Cece then she points to the goal and then to the spot in front of it and acts out like she's a defender. And Cece reacts with her whole face and body in a way that says *Me? Sweeper?*

Nelle says, "Actually I'm the sweeper."

Principal Meesley looks at her jersey and says, "Number thirteen, you're first sub," and points to the bench. Then he points at me. "Number one. Keeper."

I bite my tongue in the back of my mouth and before we go out to our new positions A brings us into a huddle and says, "We'll practice it the way he wants and if it's not working, we know our positions, and can switch it up during games. What's he going to do?"

We all nod and Jamie looks at Cece and pretends the fingers on her hands are players all lined up on the field, then acts out switching up positions. She points to her eyes and then to all of our eyes. *Pay attention. Watch each other.*

Cece smiles then reaches her hand in the middle.

"Line up! Let's go!" Principal Meesley calls.

We all reach our hands to the middle with Cece's then do our one, two, three bounces and *team*. We finish the sign, our fists closing the circle all at the same time, and even though it's silent, I swear it sounds loud.

"You all don't need a cheer for *practice*," Meesley calls.

And Georgia calls back, "Get in the spirit, Principal Meesley! We've got some games to win!"

That makes him laugh but we just keep running out to set up a ridiculous six-three-one formation, waiting to get some touches on the ball. I run past A and mutter, "This is some bullsharky," and Cece looks at us and

191

draws a question mark in the air. I point around the field at our formation then use my index fingers to make two bull horns on my head and paw my foot in the grass like I'm about to charge. Then I sign a blast from the back of my shorts. *Bullsharky.* Cece laughs and shows us the real sign for that, which looks exactly like a pooping bull and involves a blast from her elbow.

Then she throws her fingers up on her head and pretends she's a real bull. She paws her cleat on the ground and it brings up grass.

Then it catches and Quinn's doing it and Georgia and then Nelle from the bench and together we are a herd of bulls, sick of this *sharky*, ready to charge.

16

WHEN I GET HOME Cameron has his swim relay team over and they're taking up the whole kitchen, making pasta for "carbo-loading."

"You guys know my dad," Cameron says to the guys. Then Bryce comes downstairs. "And my brother, Bryce." They all say "yeah" and "hi" and then he says, "This is my relay team." Dodger and Roscoe and Fred barge in and Cameron laughs and says, "And these are our zillion pets." Then he points to me and says, "And this is Bea."

I say "hi" and "nice to meet you" but really I'm feeling weird in my own kitchen because everyone else has a title, dad and brother, and even the relay team and the dogs and Fred, and I'm just Bea.

"Bea is Louise's daughter," Cameron adds.

Bea who comes with an explanation.

They all nod like they get it now and Mom comes in and then Tucker gets home from band practice and as if our house wasn't crowded enough before, we now have nine people, two dogs, a cat, and two gigantic pots of water that are about to boil over in the kitchen.

Cameron turns down the heat and empties boxes of spaghetti into the pots and Mom gestures for me to come over so I weave a path through everyone in the kitchen and follow her to the living room.

"How was it?" she asks.

"Terrible," I say. "He wants to run a six-three-one because he thinks we don't have a chance of scoring."

Bryce escapes the kitchen too and plops down on the rug. Dodger and Roscoe sit right in his lap like they're still puppies. It kind of feels weird to talk about Meesley in front of Bryce, but I just keep telling Mom everything. I tell her about how he wouldn't listen to us about our positions and how we got old uniforms and the boys are getting new ones and he told us we could fundraise if we wanted.

I can tell that Mom's biting down hard on her tongue in the back of her mouth and then she picks up a pillow from the couch and screams into it.

Bryce and both dogs swing their heads toward Mom, but Bryce kind of looks away fast like he isn't sure he was supposed to see that, or he doesn't know what he's supposed to say so he scratches Roscoe behind the ear and gives Dodger a belly rub.

"I really have to call the school," she says. "I mean, I'm your mom."

I look right back at her and say, "I really got this, Mom. I mean, I'm your daughter."

She pulls me in for a hug and says, "Embers all right. But you just say the word," and she lifts a pretend phone to her ear.

Cameron comes in with his team and says, "We're about to watch some swim videos from practice. You all are totally welcome to watch if you want." They're holding big bowls of pasta. "There's extra in the kitchen too."

Tucker says he'll watch and Wendell sits down next to Mom on the couch and says, "Sounds interesting to me," and the swimmers all sit their long bodies down on the floor next to Bryce. He shoos the dogs to the mudroom and by the second video of Cameron flying into the wall with a two-hand touch we're all twirling spaghetti around our forks and inspecting the team's relay starts like it's the Olympics.

We watch until our bowls are empty then we leave Cameron and his teammates to themselves when they start discussing splits and times and the team that beat them last year.

Bryce goes up to his room and I wait a minute then go up too because it would feel weird to walk up right behind him, but when I get to the top of the stairs his door is open and I peek in even though I don't really mean to and he's propped up on his bed reading on the iPad with his earbuds in.

He catches my eye and looks away, but then he takes out his right earbud and says, "What?"

"What're you reading?" I ask.

He shakes his head and says, "Nothing." And I'm thinking that would be just like him, to use a teacher's iPad to pretend to read a book, but really he's watching stupid videos or listening to music instead because Bryce Valentine gets away with everything.

I turn to go but Bryce says, "*Smile.*"

"Excuse me?" I say.

"The book's called *Smile*," he says.

"Oh," I say. "Is it good?"

He shrugs his shoulders like *whatever* or *it's fine* but I know he has to like it more than that because he's reading at home.

"But I read something different in school," he says.

"Why?"

He shrugs his shoulders again and Fred hops up on his bed and snuggles around his neck like he's a scarf. "Just do."

"OK."

I turn to go to my room but Bryce calls out again. "It's about this girl who fell on her face and broke her teeth and has to do all these surgeries and stuff. And her friends are teasing her about all sorts of things."

"Sounds pretty good," I say.

"Yeah, it is. Ms. Kravitz recommended it." Then he looks down at the iPad. "Kenny and Morris say it's a girl book, though."

"That's because they share three brain cells," I tell him and I hold up three fingers like you do in American Sign Language, with your thumb.

That makes Bryce laugh, which makes me laugh a little too.

"I'm reading a book about a boy," I tell him. "His name is Jess and he likes to run and draw and his own dad makes fun of him for that and he has this best friend named Leslie, and she's a girl and their friendship is kind of like mine with Maximilian."

Bryce nods.

"And I think Jess might kind of be a bully to this one girl, but I think by the end he'll quit it because I can tell he's good."

Bryce nods again and says it sounds like a decent book.

I see the stack of notebooks on his desk and I'm

pretty sure he doesn't notice that they're out of order or anything from when I knocked them down, and I'm wondering why he keeps that picture in there and if maybe it's because it's too hard to look at and you can only do it in little bits at a time before you have to stuff it away again.

And when I look back at Bryce for a hundredth of a second I swear I can see that little baby from the photo right there in his face.

"Well, good night," he says.

"Good night," I say. And I head back to my room and take out *Bridge to Terabithia* and for some reason it doesn't feel so bad, the fact that I share a wall with Bryce Valentine.

17

GRANDMA BEA IS ALREADY sitting on the bench by the field when we're dismissed. We jog over and I introduce her to my team. She says hello to everyone and that we better not waste any time because our first game is Tuesday.

Cece holds up two fingers and circles them around the field. *Two laps.* We run together and gather for stretching at the midline. While we're reaching down past our ankles to grab the grass at our cleats, Principal Meesley comes and stands by the bench next to Grandma Bea. I crane my neck to watch him.

"I'm these girls' coach," he says.

Grandma nods and points at me. "And I'm that girl's grandma." Then she looks at him and says, "And today

I'm their supervisor."

"No," he says. "You're not. For a school activity, the supervisor has to be a school employee."

I straighten back up and walk to the bench. "You never told us that," I told him.

"You never asked," he responds.

Grandma Bea stands up next to me and gives him a glare. "That tone you're using is hogwash so you can quit that right now," she tells him, then leans in toward me for a secret Embers-girls fist bump.

Principal Meesley backs up a step and says, "I'm sorry, but those are the rules."

I'm trying to figure out how we could get everyone to my house to set up A's bounce-back net and my wobbly goal in the front yard, but we don't have enough time and my yard's too small and it wouldn't work.

Then I see Ms. Blaise walking through the parking lot and Quinn and Fern start waving her down. She waves back and starts toward us. "You girls are persistent," she says. "Another practice day!" That makes me remember our evidence projects in class. We *are* persistent and I can think of tons of examples.

I introduce Ms. Blaise to Grandma Bea, and Principal Meesley says, "I was just explaining that school activities have to be supervised by school employees."

"Got any job openings?" Grandma Bea asks.

"Because I want to supervise this amazing team." She laughs a little and looks at Principal Meesley. "You don't even have to put me on payroll."

Ms. Blaise smiles. "I'll do it," she says. "I've always got notebooks to read and lessons to plan." She pats the bag slung over her shoulder. "Plus, it's an inspiring view."

"Fine," Principal Meesley says. Then he taps his clipboard against the palm of his hand a couple of times. "I just don't want them practicing anything wrong. We got a lot accomplished yesterday and they might think they have other ideas . . ."

Grandma Bea puts her hands on her hips and says, "I don't think you have to worry one bit about a group of kids who are organizing to practice on non-practice days."

Ms. Blaise nods her head like *amen.*

Grandma Bea gives me a little smile and I tell her she can leave if she wants but she just says *hogwash* and waves me off to the field. She and Ms. Blaise sit down together on the bench and Principal Meesley goes back to the boys' field and blows his whistle for them all to gather around and get their brand-new uniforms from a cardboard box that was just delivered today. I see Kenny and Morris running in together and it takes me a second to find Bryce because he's not with them. He's jogging in from the other side of the field and he doesn't stand with them while Meesley is cutting through the tape on the box.

Bryce didn't sit with them in class today either and at first I thought that wasn't a big deal because he probably just wanted to read *Smile* on his iPad without them breathing three-brain-celled comments down his neck about how boys shouldn't want to read a book about a girl. But now they're not all three stuck together at practice either. He catches me looking at him as Principal Meesley hands him number ten and I give a little wave and he sends one back. Then I hold up the sign for three and point to my brain and then at Kenny and Morris, who are trying to juggle their soccer balls but keep losing them off their thighs after two bounces. Bryce hides a laugh behind his hand.

Today we practice making runs up the field, clapping our hands hard for the ball, or waving, and pointing to where we want the pass to go.

A and I show how a defensive back could make an overlapping run up the line around her own midfielder. "Then the midfielder drops back for support," A says.

We run wall passes, where you send it to a teammate and she one-touches it back to you up the field making a triangle. We practice moving diagonally toward the goal and sending it out to the wings and we practice getting the ball to A or me or Cara in the corners because we have good feet for crosses, and Jamie and Micah and Cece are good at rushing in from the eighteen-yard line to finish. We practice using our support back in order to find new ways forward.

Cece shows us the sign for *sorry*, a hard, fighting fist that realizes it's done wrong, making circles around your heart. And she shows us the sign for *good* and *OK* and *again* and we practice communicating on the field.

When I look up to check on Grandma Bea and Ms. Blaise, I see that Ms. Kravitz has joined them and they're all watching us play.

At the end we split into two teams for a short-sided scrimmage and when we take our positions, we put up our index-finger bull horns and paw our hooves in the grass and even Grandma Bea does it from the bench. "Charge!" she hollers. Ms. Blaise and Ms. Kravitz laugh and throw up their horns too.

While we unlace our cleats and put on our sweat-shirts, Ms. Blaise and Ms. Kravitz holler "Great practice, girls! We'll see you next time!" and start walking toward the parking lot. Grandma Bea waits while Maximilian shares our stats with us.

Number of passes: 102
Number of crosses: 6
Goals scored: 8
Goals saved: 4
Number of high fives: 12

When we huddle up, I tell them I think we need a team dinner this weekend and even though Cameron's relay team was four kids and my team is thirteen, and I haven't exactly asked my mom or Wendell, I say that we can do it at my house because I have tons of US Women's National Team games saved that we could watch to get ready for Tuesday. Nelle signs *team* and pretends to eat and Maximilian writes down *This weekend*. Cece nods. A says she'll organize and text everyone, pulling her phone from her bag.

Then we put our hands together for our cheer, and when we sign *team*, our fists closing the circle, Grandma Bea joins the huddle and points to every single one of us, even Maximilian, and makes the sign for *good*.

Grandma Bea drives Bryce and me home and comes with us inside to check on Mom. She had an appointment today and she should be resting upstairs but when we get there Mom and Aunt Tam are on the floor of Mom and Wendell's room looking at the directions for the crib with a hundred pieces and screws and tools scattered around.

Aunt Tam looks up. "I told her to wait until Wendell got home."

Grandma Bea laughs. "Well, that was your first mistake."

"But he manages a *hardware store*, Louise," Aunt Tam says.

"We don't need Wendell for this," Mom says and waves Bryce and me over. "How was practice?"

We sit down between her and Aunt Tam on the carpet and at the same time he says *fine* and I say *great*.

Then I ask her about the team dinner and she smiles and says, "Of course. I think that's a great idea." She rubs a hand over her belly.

"Was your appointment OK?" I ask.

"Yup! Baby's still in position, but staying put for now." Mom hugs us around the shoulders and says, "OK, now see if you two can find a piece labeled *D*, because that's supposed to go in here."

I look at the pictures on the instructions and Bryce spots the piece labeled *D* and Grandma Bea is gathering together the screws that hold it all together and step by step we figure it out and build the crib.

Bryce and I each pick up an end and inch it toward the wall where Mom is pointing. "Right there," she says.

Seeing the crib up and ready for a baby makes it feel more real that we're going to have another person in our family, and soon. I've been so focused on Wendell and Cameron and Tucker and Bryce and Dodger and Roscoe and Fred that I haven't really thought about my new little sibling actually being here, in the house, with us, and if I'm excited or not or what. I think I am excited but I'm also kind of not because the baby will be new, and I've had a lot of new lately.

But when I look around at Mom and Grandma Bea and Aunt Tam and Bryce and Dodger and Roscoe and the new crib, I realize I still have the old too, all blended together with the new. And that maybe the doctor is right. This baby will have a pretty great family.

Mom hugs Aunt Tam and says thanks for helping, and Grandma Bea bends down and talks to Mom's belly, "Hey there, grandchild. Don't you go getting ahead of yourself now, you hear?"

She pats Mom's belly and says, "We'll see you when it's time."

18

I WAKE UP THINKING what am I doing inviting my whole team here? Everyone knows my mom married Bryce's dad, but it's one thing to know we're a "blended family" and another thing to walk right into our house and see all the blending. And even if I've gotten a little bit used to the traffic of Wendell and Cameron and Tucker and Bryce and Dodger and Roscoe and Fred, maybe everyone on my team will have a hundred questions like, *So how many brothers do you actually have?* and, *Is your mom's baby Bryce's sibling too?* and *What do you call each other?* That last question isn't actually a bad one because I'm still working on figuring out the answer.

But before I can work myself into too much of a panic, Mom pokes her head in. "Morning, Bea. Three."

I take a deep breath. "One, that the baby's crib will be in your room." That makes Mom laugh. "Two, that I actually like reading this year. And three, carbo-loading."

"Those are great ones," she says, and kisses the top of my head.

A is the first person to get here. She walks across the street and knocks on our door, then pulls off her boots and says hi to Mom and Wendell. Cameron and Tucker are at a football game at the high school, and Bryce is up in his room with the dogs and cat, so it doesn't feel so crowded and blended and like I need to explain everything.

Micah comes in with her mom, who says hi to Mom and Wendell and thanks for hosting and how excited she is to see everyone at our first game Tuesday. Then she gives Micah a fist bump and says, "See you at eight."

Cece comes with her mom and Tess gets there a minute later with her dad. Cara and Jamie arrive together with Cara's grandma and Georgia's aunt drops her off. Everyone's family comes in to say hi to Mom and Wendell and they all ask when the baby's due and say *How wonderful!* and that they're looking forward to Tuesday and that they'll be back at eight o'clock.

I'm waiting for Maximilian to get here because I know he's worried about showing up at Bryce Valentine's house. That's why he hasn't visited. I'm sure of it. It's enough to be stuck in his class and laughed at since second grade.

But when he does get here, he doesn't knock. He just walks right through the door like he's been here a hundred times and I'm so happy I touch him on the outsides of his shoulders and say, "Thanks for coming."

His grandma pokes her head in and says, "So proud of you, Bea! Go, team!"

When everyone's arrived, Wendell heads out to pick up the pizzas and we fill the living room to watch some soccer. We squish six of us on the couch, two in the chair from the Valentines' house, and the rest on the floor. But we only stay seated for one half because we're watching the World Cup game from 2019 when the US was playing Thailand and in the second half they scored ten goals. Four of those goals were scored in a six-minute span of time. We know that because Maximilian announces it.

"Incredible!" he cheers and we're all standing up and moving around the living room like we're right on the field with them.

A also tells us there are six starters on the field who were making their World Cup debut—that means they were playing in their first World Cup ever—and that we should treat Tuesday like our World Cup debut.

Wendell comes home with the pizzas and we line up in the kitchen to put hot slices on our plates. Then we bring them back in the living room and I switch to the World Cup final game against the Netherlands.

It's hard to sit for that game too, especially the first hour when there's no score and the Netherlands' keeper is saving everything. We watch the passes and the runs and the way they communicate, and when they move the ball up the field, shoot, and the keeper makes a save we all jump up and go, "Ohhhhhh."

Bryce comes downstairs to feed Dodger and Roscoe and peeks into the living room. I can tell Maximilian sees him because he shifts his feet and stops cheering. A few of the girls notice him looking in too and I'm thinking Maximilian is going to shrink and duck out of view before Bryce can say something mean like *Why's a boy at the girls' team dinner?* or something, because that's what Kenny and Morris would do. But instead Maximilian looks right at Bryce and says, "Want to watch?"

Bryce scoffs and says, "I know how it ends."

Maximilian just shrugs. "Suit yourself." Then he takes a sip of soda and adds, "I know how the Chronicles of Narnia movies end too but I still rewatch them all the time because . . ." He pauses and looks up at the ceiling like he's trying to find the answer up there. "Well, because they're badass. That's why."

That makes the whole team erupt, Bryce too, because Maximilian doesn't say words like *badass*.

"And so is the US Women's National Team," he continues.

Cece wants to know why everyone is laughing and no one can figure out how to sign it so I point to Maximilian and do the sign for H-A-H-A with my two fingers flapping in and out from my fist like they're hysterical. Cece laughs but it doesn't feel right having her miss what was so funny and it makes me want to learn more signs so I can speak her language.

Cece points to Bryce and then gestures for him to come in. Bryce shrugs his shoulders like *why not?* and takes a seat on the floor. The dogs follow him in and half the team gets closer so they can pet them.

We get to the point of the game where Megan Rapinoe scores on a penalty kick and we all explode, and then again eight minutes later when Rose Lavelle carries the ball from midfield, fakes to the right and strikes with her left, sinking the ball into the lower right corner of the goal. Even Bryce jumps to his feet, the dogs circling around him and yipping.

By the end of the game we're all making our index-finger bull horns and pawing the living room floor with our feet. Bryce looks at us and laughs, but it's not a laugh-at-you kind of laugh. It's a you-all-are-so-ridiculous-but-good-ridiculous kind of laugh.

After the game we start talking about what we want to wear for team spirit on Tuesday. It's a school tradition that you dress up on game day. Tess thinks we should dress up in nice clothes, like skirts and blouses, and Emmie and Georgia think we should do something wacky, like tie-dye our soccer socks and wear them to school pulled up over our pants, but then Jamie says, "When are we going to have time to tie-dye?"

"Pajamas?" Fern suggests.

Maximilian asks Bryce what the boys are doing for team spirit for their game on Monday.

"I . . . I don't know yet." Then he says "bye" quick and kind of gets weird and grabs a slice of cold pizza and heads back up to his room. Everyone looks at me like *what the heck was that?* and I shrug because how am I supposed to know?

Maximilian passes a note to Cece explaining team spirit. She reads it then uses her finger to pretend she's painting her face.

"Yeah!" Quinn says. "I have face paints. I can bring them Tuesday and we can meet early outside school."

Nelle says she has face paints too and can bring them on the bus for those who can't get an early ride.

We decide on a left cheek soccer ball and say it's a

plan and put our hands in together for a cheer.

Tess's dad is the first one to get here and then Nelle's mom and Georgia's aunt. Emmie introduces us to her mom's boyfriend and I didn't know that Emmie's family was kind of blended too. Maximilian's grandma squeezes into the mudroom and everyone's spilling into the kitchen and chatting and sticking around for a few minutes.

They all start talking about Principal Meesley and how they're not so sure about him and they're wondering if he's gotten any more encouraging and if we want them to call the school. We all agree that we wouldn't have any evidence to prove he's *encouraging*, but that we've got this, and the supervised practices on Mondays, Wednesdays, and Fridays are the best.

Then they all look around at each other and my mom is pulling out a paper and they start passing around a sign-up list to supervise.

"It's OK," I announce. "Principal Meesley said it has to be a school employee so Ms. Blaise and Ms. Kravitz agreed to do it."

But it doesn't stop them all from smiling and cheering and signing up anyway. "We want to be there," Georgia's aunt says, writing her name down. "This is something exciting." And that makes my heart beat fast *team-team team-team*.

Then Cece's mom, dad, and little brother knock and come in and we all make room and say hello and Cece points to them and makes both her hands into *F*'s. Then she brings her hands around together, meeting to close the circle, just like the sign for team. *Family.*

19

WHEN I GET TO school on Monday, I see Kenny first. He has his shaggy brown hair pulled up in two pigtails and is wearing a sports bra over his number nine brand-new soccer jersey.

Then I see Morris. And Mac and Wyatt. They're wearing tutus and have lipstick smeared all over their mouths and Greg, an eighth grader from another class, has a long blond wig that he's flipping back and forth.

They're skipping down the hall, holding hands, and fake giggling and pretending to dribble soccer balls and fall all over the place, and at first I want to laugh too because they look ridiculous, but then I hear Wyatt, in a high flighty voice say, "We're the girls' team!"

Kids in the hall are cracking up and snapping the

straps of Kenny's sports bra and smacking Morris on the butt.

"Ooooo, stop it!" they flirt and slap their hands away. "I don't want to break a nail before the game!"

And I'll tell you one thing, they aren't dressed up like me one bit because if someone snapped my sports bra or touched my butt they'd be walking away holding their bloody little noses.

The bell rings and my hands clench in fists and I'm biting hard on my tongue in the back of my mouth. But then I let my tongue go and walk to Principal Meesley's office and knock. Hard.

"Busy!" he calls. But I turn the handle anyway and Ms. Landry gives me a nod like *Go on* and I can feel my team behind me, one by one, filling up his door. I tell him what I saw and how he better go out there and make them stop.

"Lipstick and sports bras?" He leans back in his swivel chair and laughs.

"They're mocking us," I say.

"Now hang on. Let's not get too emotional. I'm sure it's all in good fun."

"It's not," Jamie says.

Principal Meesley sighs. "Look, boys dressed like girls sounds ridiculous to me too and I wish they hadn't done it. But I can't make them change their clothes."

"Yes you can," Emmie says. "Last year you made Maya wear her gym sweats all day because her shorts didn't hang longer than her fingertips."

And for a second he has nothing to say, and I'm thinking he's going to take a breath and tell us *fine* and go out there and see for himself how mean the boys are being. But instead he stands up from his swivel chair and says, "Right now I have to get these morning announcements to the teachers, but I'll circle back to this when I'm done." He pushes through us and hustles down the hall and Maximilian opens the notebook and writes it all down.

When I get to homeroom, Ms. Blaise is welcoming everyone in and Ms. Kravitz has the kids on the boys' team in the little office room in the back of the class. I'm peeking through the glass panel on the door and I can see she's looking at them, each one of them.

I hear Kenny's voice say, "It's just a joke."

I'm peeking in to see what Bryce is wearing but I don't see him. He was just wearing normal clothes when we left the house this morning so I bet he's still in the locker room getting all dolled up and the thought of it makes me clench my fists again.

Georgia and A are saying, "What jerks!"

"Seriously," Tess adds. Her eyes look a little red and I bet they are because I feel like crying too.

Ms. Blaise doesn't try to quiet us. She's listening actually. And just as the boys are coming out from the back office, the classroom door opens and Bryce walks in.

At first I want to kill him because he's wearing my number one jersey and that means he went in my room without asking. But then I see he's also wearing black soccer shorts, white soccer socks pulled up and rolled down to his shin guards, his soccer sandals, a ball at his feet, and a duffel over his shoulder.

He looks like a badass soccer player.

Then Kenny says, "Wait, you dressed up like your twin?"

The boys all laugh and Bryce's cheeks turn a little red and my heart's beating a hundred miles per hour until Bryce says, "You said to dress like the girls' team. I did."

Morris rolls his eyes and says, "I think you missed the point."

Bryce's cheeks turn a brighter, hotter shade of red. Then he says, "What *was* the point?"

Ms. R points her right index finger toward her left one then draws a question mark in the air and Cece raises her hands and rotates them back and forth for applause. Then she leans in toward Kenny and Morris like she's waiting for an answer and I look at Bryce and smile.

Morris shrugs and mumbles something under his breath about Bryce going to the girls' team dinner so maybe he should just join their team too. The boys chuckle a little until Georgia looks back at Morris and says, "You might want to up your game a little before you go making fun of our team. We've seen your attempts at juggling. One-two-drop. Every time."

"Not true!" he shouts.

"Prove it," A says, pulling a ball out of her duffel and holding it toward Morris.

I'm thinking Ms. Blaise or Ms. Kravitz will tell us to cut it out and quiet down, but they don't. They're just watching and listening.

A motions the ball toward Kenny. "No takers?" Then she starts juggling right there in the middle of all the tables with her jean leggings and her blousy shirt, and she doesn't even take her eyes off the boys when she does. After fifteen she flips it up, catches it, and holds it back out. "You sure?"

The boys all grumble and smack their teeth and say they're not going to get into a competition with some girl, but the whole class knows the real reason they won't reach out for the ball.

Then I take a turn and I stop at fifteen, like A, and offer it up to the boys. They're all slumped down in their seats with their arms over their chests and now they all just look ridiculous in their wigs and sports bras. When Bryce walks by I whisper that I'm going to kill him for going in my room and he smiles.

It's quieting down and Ms. Blaise starts handing out little slips of paper and says, "Boys' team, write down why you dressed like this. Everyone else, write down how you felt when you saw your classmates dressed this way. You do not need to write your names."

Mad.

I slide my piece of paper over to Maximilian and he shows me his. *Helpless.*

Ms. Kravitz collects all our papers and reads the boys' team's first.

To be funny.
Because everyone else was.
You're taking it the wrong way.
It was Kenny's idea. But it wasn't funny.
It was a team thing.

I know which one was Bryce's. The one that said it wasn't funny. And I want to know who wrote *You're taking it the wrong way* because who are they to tell me how to take it?

Then Ms. Kravitz reads the rest of the class's slips of paper. *Sad. Helpless. Mad. Confused. Upset.*

Hurt. Ms. R brings her two index fingers up and twists them toward each other like they're really digging in.

Ms. Kravitz doesn't say anything after she reads the last one. We just sit there in silence for what feels like a hundred minutes and I'm thinking about what everyone wrote and why Bryce decided to not follow Kenny and Morris for once in his life and actually do something cool and on his own. And I'm wondering if maybe it was because he hung out for a little at our team dinner and he got to see our cheer and if that was kind of like peeking in on an in-between time. Or if something in his book, *Smile*, made him want to give up trying to be friends with jerks.

Ms. Kravitz tells us to push our tables aside and shows us how to arrange our chairs in two rows down the classroom, facing each other. Then she starts assigning seats for an activity.

"Morris, here. A, here." She points to two chairs facing each other.

"Wyatt. Bea." She points to the next two chairs and I sit down across from Wyatt, who is wearing a purple sparkly tutu over his soccer warm-ups, red lipstick, and his hair in a hundred little pigtails over his head.

"Bryce. Kenny," Ms. Kravitz continues. "Mac. Maximilian." And on down the line until we are all sitting

221

knee to knee with a classmate.

Ms. Blaise says, "Now, people on this side, you have thirty seconds to explain to the person sitting across from you how you feel."

Wyatt starts saying how it was just supposed to be a joke, and he sounds like Principal Meesley, like it's not a big deal and he just wants to forget it and move on. "It was Kenny's idea."

Ms. Blaise pushes him to say an actual feeling.

He fidgets with his tutu. "Bad, I guess," he says. "I feel bad because it was supposed to just be funny."

Then it's the other side's turn to say how we felt. "I'm mad," I tell him. "Because you were making fun of us and we're not like that, flipping our hair and wearing lipstick and falling all over the ball and stuff."

Wyatt's looking at his feet and Ms. Blaise makes him look up at me while I talk.

"Mad," I say again. "I'm still mad."

I'm trying to catch Kenny and Bryce out of the corner of my eye and listen to what Bryce is saying, something about how making fun of people didn't feel like team spirit and how we're not twins so he can quit calling us that.

Then our minute of being knee to knee is over and Ms. Kravitz asks if there's anything else anyone would like to add.

A raises her hand and says, "For the record, if any-one wants to wear lipstick, or tutus, or pigtails, that doesn't actually mean anything. They can still kick butt on the field if they want to, or not if they don't." She takes a big breath. "It's not like being into skirts and dresses or makeup or whatever else means you're the not-cool kind of girl. Girls are just cool. All of us." She sounds like a captain again and it makes me smile. "I mean," she asks, "how many of you can strike a ball out of the air in heels? 'Cause I can."

And I know that's true because I've seen it. I've seen her one-touching the ball dead-on in her front yard wear-ing all sorts of things that I'd never dream of wearing and I know her comment was meant for Kenny and Mor-ris and Wyatt and Mac and all the others, but maybe it was a little bit for me too.

Then Wyatt raises his hand and asks if he can go to the bathroom. When he comes back his face is washed and he's wearing his normal clothes. Mac shimmies out of his tutu and I can see some boys from the class next door passing by to go change too and even Kenny pulls off the sports bra and stuffs it in his backpack.

My mom, Aunt Tam, and A's mom are all on the bench ready to supervise when we get out to the field for prac-tice today.

Everyone was so excited signing up at our team dinner that we got at least two people signed up for every practice and that's not even including Ms. Blaise and Ms. Kravtiz, who are making their way from the bus lines over to Field B now.

A's mom is wearing black skinny pants and tall black boots and a long gray sweater. She has hoops in her ears and thin black lines painted around her eyes. Mom kisses the top of my head and tries to zip her sweatshirt up over the baby but it won't go. She promises she'll stay seated and try not to jump up and down or anything too wild and Aunt Tam gives me a nod like she'll make sure of it.

The boys' team is warming up for their game on Field A with Principal Meesley. Some of them still have their hair in tons of tiny little pigtails but it doesn't feel like they're making fun of us anymore and I'm wondering if maybe they like their hair like that and if girls can kick a soccer ball no matter how they look, then so can boys.

Wendell jogs up and joins Mom. The bench is in between the two fields so they can swivel to supervise our practice then swivel back to watch Bryce's game. And I'm thinking that's pretty fair. Ms. Blaise and Ms. Kravitz are doing that too, switching from the boys' game to our practice, cheering in both directions.

Aunt Tam played soccer in high school and is excited to be out on the field with us. She even brought a few extra soccer balls so we can run some drills without chasing after the balls every couple of minutes. Today we're working on finishing and Quinn is taking a turn as keeper.

Aunt Tam feeds the ball from the eighteen-yard line and we make runs, two at a time toward the goal.

Then A's mom jogs out on the field and says, "Here, try this. One of you run wide to the corner, the other to the post." She gestures for A to demonstrate with her and tells Aunt Tam to send it wide to the corner. A makes a run, collects the ball, looks up, sees her mom running to the far post, and crosses it. Then A's mom tracks the ball to the inside of her fancy left boot and sinks it in the corner of the goal.

We all cheer and line up to give it a try and after a few goals we switch keepers and A's mom takes a turn playing defense. She crouches low with one foot up and one back so we can't send it through her legs and she contains us until we can dribble a move around her or find a teammate back.

It's halftime on the boys' field and still zero to zero. We run a short-sided scrimmage with A's mom and Aunt Tam as captains and Mom cheers us on from the bench.

Then we huddle up and decide to end practice ten minutes early to watch the boys, even though we're still mad at them, and I kind of hope they all trip over the ball or shank every shot wide. But it's still zero to zero and Meesley is yelling at them from the sideline to *Be first to the ball!* and *Recover!* and we want to see what happens.

Kenny gets the ball in the midfield and looks up. Bryce gets rid of his defender and is making a run up the left wing calling for the ball but Kenny takes it on his own, trying to dribble through two players from the other team and loses it. The other team passes it up the field and gets to the eighteen-yard line. They do a wall pass around Mac and send the ball sailing into the upper right-hand corner of the goal.

Bryce slaps his hand against his thigh and yells, "I was open!"

Principal Meesley is yelling too and Kenny is hanging his head and running back to his spot in the midfield.

Wendell calls out, "Good run, Bryce!" then, "Come on, team! Plenty of time!"

But it isn't enough time and the boys lose zero to one. And I know what everyone's thinking. They're thinking about the boys' title. Their nine-year championship winning streak and how they better step it up if they're going to make ten.

We huddle before we leave and as we put our hands together and send our *T* fingers around in a circle for *team* I get butterflies in my stomach. Major butterflies with huge, frantic, flapping wings making fast runs toward goal.

Bryce goes home in Wendell's car and I hop in with Mom and I tell her everything about the boys' team spirit. The tutus and the makeup and how they flitted down the halls giggling and falling and pretending that girls were no good.

Mom's gripping the steering wheel so hard her knuckles are turning white and I tell her take deep breaths for the baby and she does.

"I can't believe . . . I just . . . What were they thinking?" she says. "What did Principal Meesley say?"

I look down at my hands. "Nothing. *It was all in good fun.*"

"Gaaaaaah!" Mom yells.

And I don't even tell her not to yell because I want to yell too and neither one of us has a pillow in the car so we just yell and yell and let it all out and we don't even care if the baby can hear us because maybe it should hear our roar.

"Did Bryce . . ."

"No," I say. "He dressed up like me. Like a badass soccer player."

Now Mom has little tears in the corners of her eyes

and it makes a big lump rise up in my throat because I'm thinking about how Bryce might have lost his friends Kenny and Morris and how I think that's not so bad because they were cruddy friends anyway, but Bryce might be sad. And he did a pretty good job of standing up, even when it was hard.

When we get home Mom pulls Bryce in and holds him in the tightest, longest hug and she's kissing his forehead and whispering that she's so grateful for him and he's not shaking her off, not even a little.

Then he hands me my jersey and I'm thinking I'm pretty grateful for him too, and maybe when Mom pulls back my comforter tomorrow morning and asks me for my three I'll say him.

20

IT'S GAME DAY AND I can't even focus on independent reading. My mind keeps running to the field, to Principal Meesley, to the other team and if they'll be good and have more than one sub or a real goalie.

I touch the soccer ball that Quinn painted on my face and I can't stop puffing out my left cheek to feel it spread and crack.

Ms. Blaise tells us it's time to find a good stopping place and I'm two pages from the end of the chapter so I try to pull my brain back to the book and keep reading about how Jess and his teacher went to Washington, DC, to look at art, which I think is maybe a little weird, but Jess is having the best day ever and since his dad thinks he shouldn't be drawing because he's a boy I'm happy that Jess has Miss Edmunds to show him that art is for everyone.

I don't make it to the end of the chapter before Ms. Blaise asks us to open up to our claim and evidence charts in our notebooks. "I want you to add the name of a character or person you're reading about. Then one trait they have."

Ms. Kravitz is kneeling down at our table and talking to Cece about a character in her book and Ms. Blaise is helping Maddie, who's reading a nonfiction book about dolphins. "Well," she whispers. "Let's write down *Dolphins* for the character."

At the end of class Ms. Kravitz tells us that we're going to be choosing a person or a character to write a paragraph about soon. We'll have a claim and use evidence to back up that idea.

Some kids groan and Ms. Blaise reminds us that using evidence to prove our claims, the things we believe, and being able to answer the question *why?* are really powerful skills.

I catch Maximilian's eye and he gives me a thumbs-up and I'm thinking Ms. Blaise has no idea that we're expert evidence collectors already.

As we're packing up, she passes a strip of paper to each of us with a sentence starter on it. "Finish the sentence and hand it to me before you leave," she says.

I straighten the strip out on my table. *I know* _____ *is a good book for me because . . .*

My mind is still hustling up the soccer field, imagining the plays and passes, and I have to work to make my brain finish the sentence.

I write:

I know <u>*Bridge to Terabithia*</u> *is a good book for me because . . . when I'm reading it I don't want to stop.*

It doesn't seem like such a big deal, but it is for me.

Ms. Kravitz looks at my sentence and gives me a fist bump. "That's great evidence," she says. Then she opens *Bridge to Terabithia* to where my bookmark is, thumbs a few pages ahead, and purses her lips. She takes a big, serious breath. "The next time you're reading," she says. "Make sure you're in a cozy, safe place."

I nod my head and remember what Cameron said about needing tissues for this book. Then she puts her hand on my shoulder and the bell rings. We all pack up and Georgia and A link my arms and we walk together to the water fountain before our next class, trying to stay hydrated for the game.

Principal Meesley is on the field before we are and as soon as we open the big, heavy school door to walk out he's already yelling at us to hurry up. We start running, duffel bags whacking our sides. The other team's bus is parked in the lot and they're passing the ball on one side of the field and taking shots on goal. Their uniforms are maroon and white and they all have matching curly maroon and white ribbons spilling from their ponytails. And I'll tell you one thing. If this had been two days ago I would have laughed at those ribbons but I'm thinking about A and her mom and a zillion other badass girls so I just let them be and start scoping out their skills.

We tie our cleats and pull up our socks and even if our uniforms are old and baggy, I know our face-painted soccer balls look good. We jog our warm-up laps together and Principal Meesley leads us in stretches.

Then he gives us a big lecture about defense. "Contain, contain. Play it safe. Don't reach for the ball. Wait for it. If you get it, boot it as far as you can."

A looks at me and rolls her eyes, because I'll tell you one thing. Neither one of us has played the *Boot it!* tactic since first grade.

The referee is calling for captains and we look at Meesley because he never assigned a captain. "We'll take turns," I say. "Today it's Nelle."

Before Meesley can say no because she's too *sensitive* to be a captain or something else ridiculous like that, Nelle smiles and jogs to the midline. We take our spots on the bench and Nelle shakes hands with the other team's captain. Then she wins the coin toss so we'll start with the ball. She jogs back and we give her high fives and put our hands in for our cheer.

Then Principal Meesley calls us out to the field in his six-three-one formation. Maximilian hands me the crumbly keeper gloves and I jog out to the goal.

I can hear Meesley calling out to the fans to remind them about his don't-talk-to-me-during-games policy. "I can get a little emotional," he announces and laughs like he has some sort of inside joke with all the grown-ups. They don't laugh back with him. "But I assure you I know what I'm doing here. Nine winning years!"

I want to shout back that the boys are so *winning* this year, aren't they? But I bite my tongue in the back of my mouth and pull on the crumbly keeper gloves.

Mom's got a camping chair set up on the sideline and Wendell and Aunt Tam are here too. Grandma Bea is chatting with Maximilian's grandparents and I can see A's mom and Georgia's aunt and Emmie's mom and her boyfriend too.

We line up the way Meesley says, stacked up on defense like we don't have a chance of scoring, but before the whistle blows we all look at each other and put up our index-finger bull horns and kick our hooves because we know this is some bullsharky and we're ready to charge.

The whistle blows and Quinn taps it to A, who passes

it back to Jamie. The other team's midfielders attack the ball, but Georgia is calling for it and pointing up the line. Jamie sends it to her and Georgia one-touches it forward but there are two defenders on Quinn and because she's our only forward, we lose the ball.

Meesley is yelling, "What are you doing? Stay in position! Get back!"

My stomach drops and my hands feel all clammy in these gloves because I don't want to let in a goal in the first two minutes. They complete two passes but A knocks it out-of-bounds and I can breathe again.

Emmie intercepts their throw in and Cece, who's in her sweeper position, starts clapping hard and making big gestures that say *Push it up! Push it up the field!* Then she makes an overlapping run from the back past Fern in the midfield. She's still clapping her hands and we're all shifting, shifting back to the positions we've practiced, to the places on the field where we know to look for each other, and when we get there it's like we click into gear and can move as a team again.

Meesley is yelling. "Back! Get back! Do you listen?" and I see Emmie's mom approach the bench but Principal Meesley reminds her, "Not during the game." I see Maximilian jotting in the notebook and I give Mom a look like *we got this*, because we do, and she nods.

Cece has the ball and dribbles a few touches and

sends it to Micah, who's pointing for it in the corner and it's just like we practiced with Aunt Tam and A's mom. Micah carries it to the corner, cuts it back around a defender, and sends it far post where Cara is running and A is hovering at the eighteen-yard line for support.

I'm out at our own eighteen-yard line, clapping my gloves and seeing the whole field out in front of me, our team pushing up and going to goal, and Principal Meesley is screaming and waving his clipboard for me to get back. "Have you lost your mind?"

That makes Mom and Wendell and some of the other fans whip their heads at him, and Mom yells that he better not say one more word about her daughter's mind. But they quickly look back at the field because the ball is sailing and Cara is right there at the post to trap it off her chest and walk it in for a goal.

I scream and run the length of the field and Maximilian and Nelle rush out from the bench and we're all in a huge huddle falling over and holding each other up. The crowd is going wild too and when I look over I see Ms. Blaise and Ms. Kravitz cheering and Cece's little brother is running wildly up and down the sideline.

Mom catches my eye and smiles and sends me a virtual Embers-girls fist bump. Then she points to her heart and then up at the sky and I know she's saying *I love you all the way up to the Care Bears.*

Principal Meesley claps his hand against his clipboard and calls, "Nice finish, Cara." Then I see him clench his teeth and he calls, "You got lucky, girls! You've got to hold your positions!"

Maximilian jots that in the notebook and the referee calls for us to line back up. Tess hollers for Nelle to come sub in and Fern says she'll take a turn in goal.

"No, no!" Principal Meesley yells and the referee raises her arms at him like *Make up your mind. Hurry.* "Fern, you stay up! Bea you're in goal! Nelle, sit back down!"

I see Ms. Blaise and Ms. Kravitz and Mom and everyone watching him, then watching us, like this is a tennis match and not a soccer game. And I hear Cece's mom call out, "Let the girls play!" but it doesn't seem like Principal Meesley is listening.

I run up the field to meet Fern and give her the crumbly gloves and I look right at Meesley like *we got this.*

"If you don't . . ."

But the whistle blows and Jamie taps it up to Micah and we're off again. Moving like a team, clapping and making runs and supporting each other back and the crowd is right there with us, drowning out Meesley's calls.

Their team scores on a free kick then A scores in the upper left-hand corner of the goal on a pass back from Jamie in the last three minutes of the game. After that goal we huddle up and decide to pull a forward back and contain on defense. "Lots of passing," Emmie says. "Let's run down the clock."

And when the end-of-game whistle blows, we scream and rush the midfield and jump together into a big, blended heap.

After we line up to high-five the other team and loosen our cleats and roll down our soccer socks, Meesley pulls us to the middle of the field and gives us a big lecture about holding our positions and listening to him and he's the coach and he knows best and how we got lucky this time but he expects us to stay in our places. He holds up his clipboard showing us the six-three-one with two sweepers and one forward.

"But we won," Quinn protests.

"And we pulled it back on defense when we needed it," Emmie says.

Then Maximilian adds, "It wasn't luck," and holds up our stats from the game.

Us:	Them:
Shots on goal: 8	Shots on goal: 4
Goals scored: 2	Goals scored: 1
Goals saved: 3	Goals saved: 6
Number of subs: 4	Number of subs: 8

"We just outplayed them today. Numbers don't lie."

Principal Meesley looks at the stats and says, "The next game won't be the same."

Quinn scoffs and says, "You mean, you already think we're going to lose?"

"If you don't listen again, I would bet on it."

I catch Maximilian's eye and we all shake our heads and start walking back to the sideline where our families are waiting. Mom kisses me on my sweaty forehead. "Your soccer ball is running," she says, swiping her finger through the smudged face paint. "I'm proud of you. I'm proud of all of you."

We turn toward the parking lot and I mumble, "I wish Principal Meesley were proud." And the second I say it I feel bad because he's a cruddy coach but for some reason I still want him to think I'm good.

Mom stops and puts her hands on my shoulders. "You," she says, looking right into my eyes, "are something to be proud of. This team is something to be proud of. And you do not need that man to tell you that."

And that feels just as good as the win.

That night, I pull out *Bridge to Terabithia* and get comfortable under Mom's old comforter on my bed. I remember what Ms. Kravitz said about reading the next part in a safe place and before I even start my heart is beating fast like we're still in the last three minutes of the game and holding on, together, until the end.

And then I read it. And my reaction is the same as Jess's. *No.* Because it can't be true, and I haven't always been the best reader so I think maybe I got it wrong but I can't bear to go back and reread the sentences again so I just close the book.

It knocks the breath right out of my lungs and stings, stings like a soccer ball struck hard against cold skin, except eventually your breath comes back and the sting fades as you run it off. And the sting of a soccer ball never makes me cry.

I hold the book and I cry. And I can't stop. I cry for Leslie and for Jess and I feel a big, aching sadness. A huge, painful injury. A deep, deep loss. A loss I've never felt before and could never even imagine until now.

And when I look down at the cover with watery eyes, I read the author's name: *Katherine Paterson.* And I'm mad. I want to yell at her, argue the call, get a red card, and get ejected from all this aching hurt. I'm mad at her for making me love them so much. It feels unfair so I shake the book and pretend it's her. *Why?*

But then I'm hugging the book again, hugging it hard, because it also feels like she looked me straight in the eyes and told me the truth and didn't lie to me with happy, perfect endings for everyone.

My door clicks open. It's Bryce, and before I can shout at him to get the heck out he says, "You can borrow these guys. They help." I try to wipe my tears but I can't because they're coming too fast and in wiggle Dodger and Roscoe. Then my door closes again and the dogs hop on my bed and circle around me and put their heads on my chest right where my tears are splashing big drops. I put my arms around them and their heartbeats make mine slow and I open the book again and read it all. About the building of bridges and the making of queens. And when I finish I hold the dogs close to the ache in my chest. Then I return them to Bryce on the other side of my wall.

21

PRINCIPAL MEESLEY WAS WRONG. We won the next game of the season. Then we tied one and lost one, which was enough to earn us a spot in the playoffs. The boys' team won a couple of games, but was knocked out in the first round because Kenny learned too late that he has to pass the ball to win. We're advancing to the semifinal round. Their streak is over.

At school Kenny and Morris try to blame their loss on us. "Coach only gave us three practices a week . . ." but before they can even finish their whiny thought A puts up her hand like a stop sign. *Don't even.*

And I say, "He only gave us two, and we're doing OK." That shuts them up pretty fast. I want to tell them that practices with Meesley are actually cruddy and maybe they should have quit complaining and organized better, or passed the ball to their teammates, but I just bite my tongue in the back of my mouth because we have games to win and I don't have time for them.

Now that the boys are out, we have to have practice every day with Principal Meesley. But each day we get more supervisors too.

He tried to tell them it was unnecessary now that he would be there every day, but A's mom responded, "We appreciate being involved."

They stand on the sideline during practice and it feels pretty good, like they're reminding Meesley that they're there. For us. Plus, when he leaves at four thirty, we all stay until five to practice for real.

Ms. Blaise and Ms. Kravitz still come sometimes, but we've also had Maximilian's grandma, and Fern's uncle. Jamie's older brother, Quinn's stepdad, and Cara's "big sister" from her mentor program. Sometimes we have a whole bench of supervisors.

And each game we get more fans. Maximilian is keeping track in the notebook. Last game, Cameron and Tucker and Bryce came, and Maddie from class brought her two little brothers. Ms. R has come to the last three games and Aunt Tam and Grandma Bea haven't missed one yet. And they're all coming to the next game. The semifinals. Tomorrow.

Wendell says he's going to leave work early today to supervise practice even though I tell him he doesn't have to. But he says he wants to be there, and he will be there. And after school when the bells rings and we rush to the field, he is.

And so is Micah's mom and Cece's mom and Tess's dad.

And when Principal Meesley leaves at four thirty, we run drills with three forwards heading toward goal, making runs wide, and covering each other back.

Then at the end, we throw our hands in the middle for a cheer. Supervisors and all.

Maximilian packs up the balls and I loosen my cleats and Wendell says, "See you at the condos."

I look at him. "Thanks," I say.

Ever since I finished *Bridge to Terabithia* I've been walking home with Maximilian along our tramped-down path and Wendell has picked me up there because that feeling of loss still sits heavy in my belly, right mixed in with all the sparking embers. And the last thing I need is Maximilian hustling through the woods alone to make it home before dark and tripping on a thick tree root, because all I can pick up on the walkie-talkie is static. Plus, it feels good. To walk down our path together, past our perfect climbing tree, and out into the yards behind the condos. To go right in through his door and hear his grandma say *Mi casa es tu casa*. And to hear Wendell's honk-honk and then climb in with him and drive home.

When we get back to the house and open the door, I hear a baby crying. I drop my duffel and Wendell drops the car keys and we rush into the living room. "Louise?"

"Relax, relax. It's Cameron's."

Then Cameron comes around the corner with a plastic baby and Wendell and I can't help it. We start cracking up.

"It's not funny!" Cameron says. "The thing won't stop crying ever!"

The doll's onesie is unsnapped and Cameron is sticking the key that's zip-tied to his wrist in the keyhole in the doll's back. "I have to hold it for two minutes. If it stops crying, then great. If not, I have to click it to another position and hope that works."

Wendell and I can't stop laughing and we kind of get Mom going too and Bryce rushes downstairs and even though he's laughing he takes the baby from Cameron and holds it in the crook of his arm. Then he pulls Cameron over by the zip-tied key, shifts the baby to his shoulder, and puts the key gently into the baby's back. Cameron rolls his eyes and holds his arm still while Bryce rocks the doll.

"It doesn't care if you rock it like that," Cameron says.

Then the baby stops crying and Bryce smiles up at him and says, "Maybe it does care."

Cameron takes a deep breath then tucks the doll under his arm and walks upstairs to his room, calling down, "Did you know the computer records how long the baby is held? I just want to put it down already! This is the worst project . . ."

"Maybe it'll record that you're holding it in a headlock!" Bryce calls upstairs.

Then we hear Cameron's door close and we all try to stop laughing but we can't until Mom rubs her hand over her belly and says, "The real baby is kicking if anyone wants to feel."

Wendell puts his cheek down and says, "Give me a kick!" and the baby does and Wendell pretends to fall to the floor.

"Definitely an Embers," I say, sitting next to Mom, and she gives me a secret Embers-girls fist bump.

Then Wendell goes to start dinner in the kitchen and it's my turn to put my hand on Mom's belly. I wait for a kick and feel the baby dig its heel into my palm. I smile at Mom and Bryce puts his hand in too and we wait for another kick together and while we're sitting there like that, with our hands in, it feels a little like our team cheer.

Then we get a kick and we both jump a little.

"That's awesome," Bryce says.

"I think so too," says Mom.

At dinner we all scooch a little closer and Mom sets up the high chair at the corner between Cameron and Wendell for the plastic baby. As soon as we sit down and Wendell scoops heaps of steaming spaghetti casserole on our plates, the baby starts crying.

"That's how it always goes," Wendell says. "Right when you sit down . . ."

Cameron picks the baby up and puts the key in its back but it gets louder after two minutes so he clicks it to the next position. "I swear every time I put it down it starts crying."

"So don't put it down," Mom answers.

At first we start laughing but then we realize she's not kidding and I picture her and Aunt Tam side by side, walking me through the night, laps and laps around the condo's backyard.

Wendell chuckles and he starts to say he'll never forget those days for any of his boys, but his voice is all shaky.

The doll stops crying and Cameron takes the key out of its back. He holds it for a minute and takes a few bites of spaghetti casserole over the doll's head. "I mean,

I know we did this when Bryce was a baby, but this thing's not even real!"

Tucker starts snickering. "Remember Christmas Eve?"

They all laugh, even Bryce, because they must have told him this story a hundred times already. But I've never heard it.

"It was Bryce's first Christmas so he was already ten months old, but he was getting teeth and he just wouldn't sleep. Every time Dad would lay him down in his crib he'd just start crying until he picked him up again," Cameron starts.

Then Tucker says, "But Cameron and I were worried that we wouldn't be sleeping when Santa came and he'd skip our house because of that song, *He sees you when you're sleeping . . . He knows when you're awake . . .*"

"We tried putting pillows over our heads and stuffing socks in our ears, but Bryce just kept wailing," Cameron continues. "Then we heard Dad crying too. Quiet cries, though. Not like Bryce."

"I was so tired," Wendell adds. His eyes are watery from laughing and remembering.

They tell the rest of the story and even though they're laughing, the story hits me deep down in that aching place and it makes a lump rise up in my throat that makes it hard to swallow.

Finally Cameron and Tucker gave up on Santa and knocked on their dad's bedroom door and said they'd take a turn walking the baby. Bryce was already heavy by ten months and it took them both to walk and rock him around and around their bedroom.

"But then I swear we heard jingle bells outside," Tucker says. Cameron nods and my mom looks across the table at Wendell and smiles.

Bryce finally fell asleep while his brothers walked and shushed and then they counted on their fingers *one, two, three* and lay back in Cameron's bed with Bryce in their arms and slept. All three of them.

"And," says Tucker, "our stockings were full in the morning."

"It was our first Christmas without Mom," Cameron says. "But our first with Bryce."

And just when Wendell is about to get all cry-snorty the fake baby starts up again and it cuts through that achy place and makes us all laugh a little, and I'm thinking that if the loss of a character from a book still sits hard in me, what kind of ache must live deep inside all the Valentines.

After dinner Mom runs downstairs and gets the baby front-pack carrier that we picked up at a yard sale before we moved and shows Cameron how to put it on and tighten the straps.

"It'll be a little big, but it'll free up your hands and the baby will still be held," she explains.

"Are babies really like this?" Cameron asks. "Like, they know how much they've been held and how long it takes for someone to pick them up when they start crying?"

Mom nods her head and I'm wondering if that's true. If our hearts are like little computers that record when we've been held and soak up all the feelings around us and tick the seconds until we're picked up in safe arms. Arms like Wendell's. Arms like Cameron's and Tucker's. And Grandma Bea's and Mom's and Aunt Tam's. And I'm thinking that maybe having more players on your team is OK. And maybe it isn't an accident that the sign for *team* and the sign for *family* look the same, big wide circles holding everyone in.

22

OUR SEMIFINAL GAME IS at the other team's field, and they have fancy bleachers for the fans. Their side is full of people climbing the stairs and finding their seats, and even though it's a twenty-minute drive, our side is full too.

Ms. R, Ms. Blaise, and Ms. Kravitz are all here. And Wendell and Mom and Cameron, with the fake baby in the front-pack carrier on his chest, and Tucker and Bryce and A's mom and Cece's family and Maximilian's grandparents and a hundred other people who are all cheering for us.

When we get off the bus A tells me that if we make it to the finals her dad is coming from Brooklyn to watch.

"That's great," I say, but she just kind of shrugs like it's no big deal.

The other team is warming up on one side of the field. When we played them in the regular season we tied 1–1. Cara scored the goal on a run from the midfield just like Rose Lavelle in the World Cup Final. The other team scored their goal from a wall pass around our defender and a strong finish into the corner of the net. They're good.

But so are we.

"We're going back to a defensive lineup," Meesley says. "Two sweepers. One striker . . ."

We groan and protest but he cuts us off and says, "I got you this far, didn't I? Trust me."

We all look around at each other, and I say, "Um, no. *We* got us this far."

Principal Meesley looks up at me, then to A and Cece and Tess and Emmie and around our whole circle. "It's been an impressive season," he says. And for one minute I'm thinking he really sees us, but then he starts listing off the same old defensive positions, and Maximilian hands me the cruddy goalie gloves.

When the referee calls the captains for a coin toss, A points at Cece and pretends to flip a coin off her thumb. Cece smiles and runs out toward midfield. Principal

Meesley calls after her like she can hear him and then he runs and puts his hand on her shoulder and shakes his head no. He waves A over instead.

But A signs *no*.

The referee blows her whistle like *Hurry up* and Meesley waves Emmie over, but she signs *no* too.

"She knows how to do a coin toss," Micah yells. "Let her go."

Cece gives him a good, hard glare like he better quit looking down at her like that, then she trots off to the midline to shake hands with the other team's captain. When the coin is in the air she pats her head and the referee nods and catches the coin. Heads. Cece turns to us and rotates both her hands in applause. Our team is starting with the ball.

We do our cheer and run to our places on the field.

"All efforts on defense!" Meesley yells. "Stay in position!"

And he means it because the second Quinn sees an opening and makes a run he yells at her and the next time the ball goes out, he subs Nelle in and pulls Quinn off the field.

"When you start listening . . ." I hear him say.

Then Micah tries to take the ball from one of their forwards and she misses and hustles to recover back but Principal Meesley is calling, "Don't reach!" Then he shakes his head and slaps his clipboard and yells, "So slow!"

Maximilian jots it down and there's a roar from the crowd. A big, fierce roar because it seems like the better we get, the closer we get to the finals, the worse Principal Meesley acts. Even the coach for the other team walks over to him and the referee gives him a warning.

Micah's mom is on her feet like she doesn't give a *sharky* about his don't-talk-to-me-during-the-game policy and she's ready to go down there and give Meesley a piece of her mind.

Principal Meesley subs Micah out and sends Quinn back in, pointing his thick finger too close to her face as a warning to stay in position out there. He doesn't say anything to Micah when she reaches the sideline, just points to the bench.

And there's a fire in my belly. Not just because he's yelling, but also because he isn't letting us play. He's not letting us try to recover and support each other. He's not letting us spread out and make runs and move together. As soon as someone steps out of line he yanks them out and we're all just playing flat defense and booting it out when we get a chance. Booting it to no one. Like we're scared.

We are not scared.

Mom gets up from her seat and walks down the

steps and onto the sideline. Principal Meesley sees her and nods like *OK, OK, I see you. I'll tone it down.* Then he waves his clipboard. "Not during the game." Mom shakes her head and I can see her biting her tongue in the back of her mouth and I give her a look like *I got this.* She puts her hands beneath her belly and waddles back up the stands.

Nelle tries to clear a ball after Meesley yells, "Boot it!" but it bounces back off one of their forwards and their other forward follows it in and taps it around me and into the goal and it's 0–1 and Principal Meesley is shaking his head.

All our families and teachers and classmates are telling us it's OK and we can do it.

And they're right. We got this. But we can't win with him.

So I call everyone in and we circle up, tight and locked, like the sign for *team*, and I look at each one of them in the eyes and I know deep down in the embers of my gut that we have to do something. Do something big so he can't keep yanking us out and pushing us back and telling us to quit reaching and quit running and quit moving forward, together. Even if it costs us the game. Even if it costs us the season.

I'm thinking of Mom and how she said that this team is something to be proud of, and I'm tired of waiting for

Meesley to realize that. "Follow my lead," I say. And I take off my goalie gloves and walk to the bench. I sit down and I unlace my cleats.

"What are you doing?" Meesley says. "Get out there!"

A sits next to me and unlaces her green Diadoras and pulls down her soccer socks. Micah and Emmie and Jamie sit and pull their jerseys off over their heads to the T-shirts beneath.

Principal Meesley is clapping his hands in front of our faces like he's trying to wake us up. "Come on! What are you doing?"

Our whole team is off the field and the referee is blowing her whistle and the fans are whispering and waiting.

"You have one minute to get lined up or we call the game!" the referee tells us and the other team is all staring at us, hands on hips.

I push my soccer socks down over my shin guards and look up at Meesley. "I'm not playing unless you leave."

"Me either," says A.

"What?" he says. "Get back out there . . ."

"We'd rather forfeit than play for you."

He shakes his head and taps his hand against his clipboard. "I knew you were quitters," he mumbles.

I point to the fence just beyond the bleachers.

255

He looks up at the fans and takes a big, deep, dramatic breath like he's going to calm down now. Then he smiles like everything is cool.

Everything is not cool.

"Come on, girls," he says.

And then it really is like one of those sports movies where everyone stands up until they get their team back because Cece points toward the fence too. Then Emmie and A and Micah and Maximilian and all thirteen of us.

And then some of the kids from our school starting cheering. Clap. Clap. Clap. And even a few of the girls from the other team point toward the fence and for a minute it doesn't feel like we're opponents at all.

"You can't play without a coach. League rules," Meesley says, and he looks at the referee who's jogging toward our sideline. She nods her head like that's true and blows her whistle and says loud enough for everyone to hear that she'll give us one more minute to take the field *with* a coach.

Then Aunt Tam stands up and says, "I'm these girls' coach." And A's mom does too. And Ms. Blaise and Ms. Kravitz and Grandma Bea and Ms. R all say *Me too* and before we know it we have a hundred coaches and they all walk down and stand by us on the bench.

The referee looks at Ms. Blaise's school employee ID and nods like that works for her and blows her whistle

for the game to resume. We look up at Principal Meesley and he looks at us and the fans in the stands. Then
Aunt Tam steps toward him and nods for him to follow
her. "Come on," she says and gestures toward the fence.
"Time to go."

He takes one more glance at me, then A, and Cece.
We don't look away.

Then he huffs a big breath, drops his clipboard, and
follows Aunt Tam to the fence. When he gets there he
slams his back into it hard so the chain links rattle and
he crosses his arms over his chest.

And the crowd goes wild.

Aunt Tam leans into the fence next to Meesley and
gives me a look like *I got this* and I send her one right
back. Then we lace up our cleats, pull together for a cheer,
and run out to our positions as a team. Then we throw
our bull horns up and kick our hooves and when we look
up, all our coaches are pawing right along with us.

A gives me a smile from center midfield, and I'm
thinking it's probably good she moved from Brooklyn to
Evergreen Road.

The whistle blows and Cara taps it up to Jamie, who
dribbles it a couple of times and sends it to me. I'm looking up at who's there and I see my team—making runs,
getting open, clapping their hands, pointing to holes in
the field. I hear them behind me too and when Quinn

claps and loops a run around, I send it up and stay back for support, following her up the field.

We're moving as a team again and Nelle is telling us to "Push it up! Push it up the field!" and I can see Principal Meesley take a step from the fence like he's about to yell for us to *stay back!* but Aunt Tam steps up too and holds out her finger like *don't you dare.* He shakes his head and sinks back into the fence.

Grandma Bea is waving her arms toward goal. "Go! Go!" she calls. A has the ball and I'm running toward the eighteen-yard line. A defender approaches her fast and I clap my hands and point. She sends a short pass, which I one-touch past the defender and right back to A's left foot. She dribbles once and shoots and I think I hear Mom scream out a cheer before the ball even hits the back of the net.

We rush A and scream and rotate our hands in applause.

But when our huddle breaks and we're heading to line up again I see Mom on the sideline, hunched over with her hand on the back of the bench, calling for Wendell in the stands, her other arm folded beneath her belly. Cameron and Tucker and Bryce are rushing down and with my heart still beating fast from the goal, I run too. Right off the field and to my mom.

Tess subs in for me and the game starts up and

Wendell holds Mom around the shoulders and says, "It's OK. Bea, you stay. Play. Win."

But when she takes a step toward the parking lot I can see her water's broken. The baby's coming. Coming early. Wendell's voice shakes and Bryce doesn't know what to do with his hands without Dodger and Roscoe to fill them, and Aunt Tam and Grandma Bea are telling Mom to breathe and that everything is going to be great.

"I'm coming," I say, and I look up at A on the field and A's mom on the sideline and they look back at me like *We got this.*

They don't make Mom fill out any paperwork this time because every two minutes Mom doubles over and grunts and tries to breathe and squeezes Wendell's hand, and then it passes and she straightens back up and huffs deep. She doesn't even protest when they give her a wheelchair and push her to a room, and she doesn't let go of Wendell's hand the whole time.

Then we're all just standing there in the waiting room, Grandma Bea, Aunt Tam, Cameron and Tucker and Bryce and me, when the doll on Cameron's chest starts crying. The nurses look up and Cameron tries to explain about his class and they start laughing a little and say, "Good luck with that!"

Cameron unsnaps the baby front-pack carrier and

puts the key in the doll's back. He walks and shushes and I'm wondering what that little computer is recording. I'm watching him walking around like that, and even though he's almost six feet tall and has those long butterfly arms, I can see his toothless grin from that photo in Bryce's room and imagine him, and Tucker, walking and shushing their baby brother.

The doll quiets and Cameron takes the key out and straps the baby back in the front-pack carrier and Grandma Bea pats him on the shoulder and then she starts laughing. Those big snorting laughs that are hard to stop and her eyes are leaking little tears. "This family . . ." she starts, but she can't get it all out. I think I get what she's saying though. Because I start laughing too. I think she means, *of course the baby's coming early and it's during Bea's big game and we have a plastic doll crying in the waiting room and six people and this is all actually pretty calm because the pets aren't even here.*

Laughing so hard makes me cry too and I'm glad for that because I actually just feel like crying and laughing is a good excuse. But really I'm crying for Mom and the baby and hoping this isn't too early, and what that might mean. And I'm crying for *Bridge to Terabithia*, which I can't get out of my gut, and for the picture tucked in Bryce's notebook in his messy room on the other side of my wall, and because this year we got a team. We made a team. And how it wasn't even hard to leave the field because Mom is my first teammate and those eleven girls and Maximilian all have my back.

Aunt Tam is laugh-crying too and she grabs my hand and pulls me close and I lean my head into her shoulder as we walk circles and circles around the waiting room. "I got you, little Bea."

And then we all wait. Leaving no seats empty between us. Slumped and leaning and holding and shushing and walking and walking and walking, until we see Wendell.

As soon as he sees us he snorts once, then again, and his shoulders start to shake and the ache in my belly twists as he cries. We rush to him and he snorts and sobs and then kind of laughs a little and sputters, "They're OK. They're great."

We all have to wash our hands up to our elbows and when we go in Mom is sitting up in a hospital bed with the baby asleep on her chest. We all kind of tiptoe through the door but she waves us over so we shuffle in fast and surround the bed and Mom scooches up a little more and pulls the swaddle blanket down so we can see in.

"Two hours after we got here and there she was," Mom says. "Definitely an Embers."

I sit on the edge of the bed and look in at the baby. She

is so tiny. Five pounds, eight ounces, which the nurses say is very good, considering she was early. "She might be small," they say, "but she's strong." The shot Mom got when she was here last must have helped the baby's lungs because she doesn't have to go in one of those special plastic cribs to protect her and help her grow, but the doctor says she needs to have her skin on Mom's skin for as much of the day and night as possible. "It's the best cardiorespiratory stability you can offer her," she says, which is basically fancy hospital words for saying that Mom can make the baby's heart and lungs stronger just by holding her close.

Mom pulls me in and kisses the top of my head. "Her name's Val," she says. "Val Embers." She looks up at Wendell, who is starting to get snorty again. A blend, I think. Val for Valentine. And Embers, sparky and glowing and ready to ignite, like us.

"Don't you love her?" Mom asks.

"All the way up to the Care Bears," I tell her.

Cameron takes the doll from his chest, wraps it in an extra sheet from the bottom of the hospital bed, and starts to take it to the bathroom. "I'm not letting this thing start crying and wake up the real baby."

Mom laughs and says it's OK, that this little girl will be growing up in a house full of voices and noises and emotions so she better get used to it. But Cameron still swaddles the doll up tight, puts it in the shower stall in the bathroom, and closes the door.

Val wakes up anyway and starts crying and wants milk, but even after that she's still got her hands in little fists, wailing. So we all take turns, walking and shushing around the room, and when it's my turn, Wendell hands her to me, and she settles into the crook of my arm and she feels even smaller than she looks. And I walk her and tell her a story about a zebra and a kitty cat and a fox and an iguana, and even though they don't all seem like they belong together, they build a fort and live each day in the magic of the forest.

I walk her until she stops crying and when the nurse comes to take her for a blood test I give her a secret little Embers-girls fist bump and a look that says *you got this*.

Wendell goes with the baby and another nurse comes in to check my mom's temperature and give her a pill. "You all must be Val's brothers and sister."

I'm looking up at Mom to see if she says *well, half* or something else, but Tucker nods and says, "Yeah, she's our sister." I nod too because there wasn't anything about holding Val that felt half. And Cameron and Tucker and Bryce feel like more than half too, and not just because they added seven and we added two. And they don't feel *step* either, like they just stepped in as substitutes, or they're a step away from us. Maybe they're even starting to feel like brothers. I know for sure they're feeling like family. Like teammates.

After the nurse takes Mom's temperature and blood pressure she says Mom's OK to get up slowly from the bed to go check on how Val's blood test is going.

"I miss her already," Mom says. And I know what she means because I do too. I hold the door open for Mom and look across the hall into the nursery where the nurse is pricking Val's heel. The baby is crying, her small face pressed into Wendell's chest, skin to skin beneath his unbuttoned shirt. He kisses the top of her head and opens his arm for Mom to sit next to them. Mom holds out her finger and Val grabs on.

Right then the doll's muffled, mechanic cries make their way through the bathroom door and Cameron rushes to pick it up and get the key in its back so its little computer will record that he was a good caregiver, not one who would wrap a baby in a sheet and leave it in a shower stall behind a closed door. He's walking the baby and trying a different position with the key and we all get to laughing again.

Grandma Bea pulls a pack of M&M's from her purse and passes them around, then checks the messages on her phone. She plays one from Maximilian's grandma on speaker.

We won.

It was a late-game goal from Cece, who clapped her hands and pointed for Micah to send it through two defenders in the eighteen-yard box. Cece tapped it in the corner, and Principal Meesley stayed by the fence the whole rest of the game, and we're headed to the finals tomorrow.

23

GRANDMA BEA STAYS WITH us while Mom and Wendell and Val are in the hospital. She stays right in my room, right in my bed, and even though I'm not one for sharing, I don't mind sharing with Grandma.

In the morning of the final game she nudges me awake. "Bea, three."

I rub my eyes and clear my throat. "One, everyone comes home tomorrow. Two, that Cameron's done with that fake baby project. Three, M&M's for breakfast?"

Grandma smiles then counts out on her fingers, "One, you. Two, you. And three . . . M&M's for breakfast."

We both laugh and pull back the covers to get ready for the day. Grandma goes downstairs to start breakfast and I put on my uniform, which we're wearing today for team spirit. Cameron has morning practice so he's already gone but Tucker and Bryce are hustling down the stairs with their backpacks.

Breakfast is frozen waffles and Grandma has an M&M stuck in each hole.

"Syrup?" she asks.

Bryce laughs and shakes his head, but Grandma puts the jug out on the table anyway. "Just in case."

We go through a box and a half of waffles and a hundred scoops of yogurt then we run upstairs to brush our teeth and head out the door to the bus. Grandma Bea gives me a fist bump and says she'll see me later and that I can go ahead and start calling her Coach.

We're all so nervous for the game that even reading time in Ms. Blaise's room is hard. Even Maximilian is squirming a little in his seat. I take his T-84.

OK?

Court date. Grandparents can't come to game.

I whisper "sorry," because court days are hard for Maximilian. His mom is there and even though he doesn't have to go to the court anymore, it makes him think about her, and thinking about her is like having to do two left-foot steps in a row or getting stuck in a chair that's an odd number away from the door, and I know it'll be bothering him when his grandparents aren't at the game this afternoon.

Grandma Bea will send them a halftime update, I write and slide the calculator back to him. He smiles.

I spend most of the rest of reading time looking through the book bins, but I'm just flipping through the covers and not even really looking because I'm thinking about the start-of-game whistle blowing.

Bryce finishes *Smile* on the iPad in class and he finds the paperback copy in Ms. Blaise's library and hands it to me. "Want to read it?"

I take it from him and say thanks. I haven't started another book since I slid *Bridge to Terabithia* back on Cameron and Tucker's shelves. I've been reading articles that Ms. Blaise keeps in a special magazine bin in the back of the room. One of the old *Sports Illustrated* issues has a story about a soccer player named Ally Sentnor, who was the SportsKid of the Year and I read that one twice before I passed it on to A and Cece. I think Georgia is reading it now.

I scooch down in my chair, cross my legs at the ankles, lean *Smile* on the edge of our table, and try to start reading. It's actually pretty easy to get into and when Ms. Kravitz says it's time to find a good stopping place, I groan along with everyone else and nod a quick *thanks* to Bryce. When we're putting our books away I ask A if her dad is going to be at the game and she nods.

We spend the rest of class talking more about making an argument and using evidence. Ms. Blaise shows us lots of examples in her own notebook and then she asks us if she thinks what we're reading makes an argument, or a point. "What do you think the author believes?"

I think about Katherine Paterson and how I'm pretty sure she believes that life is fragile and you should spend it doing what you love even if other people think you should be doing something else. I think she believes in kindness and friendship and that kids can handle the truth, even the big, hard, horrible truths, because some kids are living achy like that already.

The bell rings and Ms. Kravitz reminds us that our paragraphs are due tomorrow and we should be thinking about them. "A claim about a person or character you know and three pieces of evidence."

Ms. Blaise says she's excited to see our work, and then she looks out at the whole class and says, "And we'll all be cheering for our girls' team today in their final match. Go get 'em."

In math class, Mr. Henny has a bunch of word problems on a handout and I'm about to say there's no way I'm doing all these because my brain can't do anything but think about the game, but then I see that all the problems are about our team and how many goals we'll score per minute. He says we can work in groups so I team up with Maximilian and Cece and even Bryce kind of scooches his chair up toward our table and we work through the first problem, which has us winning the game 3–1.

The rest of the day goes by slower than any other day ever. I watch the clock in every class, even lunch and recess, and when the end-of-day bell finally rings we all gather in the hall so we can walk out to the field together. Maximilian is emptying his backpack looking for the team notebook. "I must have left it in Mr. Henny's class? Or maybe in the lunchroom?" He takes a deep breath and counts eight, sixteen, twenty-four, and he looks calm. "I'll find it." I tell him I can come with him but he says it's OK and I should go warm up and then he does a little wiggle dance. "Plus I have to pee anyway." I laugh and tell him we'll see him out there.

It seems like the whole school is emptying out to the field with us. All the teachers and students, Ms. R, Ms. Landry, and even the woman from the lunchroom, and Mr. Duff, who always leaves the building right at three o'clock because he has a new baby at home, runs out quickly at the end of the day, but then comes back to the field carrying his baby in a click-out car seat.

It makes me think of Mom and Val and how they're coming home tomorrow as long as Val passes some tests and I'm so excited for that too and it's getting all mixed up in my belly with my game nerves and I just can't stand still.

Ms. Blaise and Ms. Kravitz are here and Laurel and Maddie from class and even most of the boys' team, including Bryce, though I don't see Kenny and Morris so maybe they got on the bus home, and I'm pretty certain the only person left in the school is Principal Meesley, sitting in his office with his *Do Not Disturb* sign.

A points out her dad on the sideline. "Are you going to go say hi?" I ask. She gives him a little wave and he blows her a kiss.

"No," she says. "Later."

Grandma Bea is Coach today. And A's mom. And Aunt Tam and Georgia's aunt and Nelle's mom and all the people who stood on our sideline and supervised our practices and cheered us on and believed in us.

Wendell is here and I run to him before we warm up. He says Mom and Val are doing great and sending me big Embers-girls fist bumps and that they'll see me tomorrow. Thinking about them, walking and shushing around that hospital room, makes my heart beat *team-team team-team* and in my head I dedicate this game to them.

The team gets together to jog our warm up laps and when we do A says to me, "The last time he came was to

271

finalize some things for the divorce." I slow my stride so she has more time to tell me anything else if she wants.

"I'm sorry," I say.

"Mom said she wanted space and wanted me, and told him about moving to Vermont and Dad said great, like it didn't even matter to him that she was taking me with her."

We slow toward the end of the lap and circle up to stretch.

"So, anyway, that's my dad. I kind of half miss him and half hate him." I put her hand on my shoulder and pretend it's to hold my balance while I'm pulling my other leg back to stretch my quad, but really, I hope it feels like a sort-of hug, like a Maximilian hug. An I-hear-you hug.

The other team has purple and white uniforms and five substitutes and when they jog it's in two straight lines and they sing chants while they warm up.

When the referee calls for captains A says it's my turn and everyone nods so I run to the midfield and shake their captain's hand. She's taller than I am, and wearing number ten, and flipping her orange mouth guard on and off her teeth. She calls "tails" when the coin is in the air but when it lands back in the referee's palm and she slaps it on the back of her hand, it's heads. We win the toss and we start with the ball.

Grandma Bea calls us together and we all put in a hand and start our one, two, three bounces and *team*. Then we take the field and the whistle blows and it doesn't even seem real, all the fans cheering and the ball rolling from foot to foot and the clap-clap-claps and quick runs, and how we're playing in the finals and Principal Meesley is all alone in his little office in his empty school.

We're not even five minutes into the game when I remember Maximilian.

I look at the bench and see our coaches and Tess but he's not there. My heart beats that *team-team* and Aunt Tam is giving me a look like *What's wrong?* so I call out "Maximilian?"

I run close to the sideline and she says she hasn't seen him, but Emmie's making a run up the opposite wing and I need to recover to the middle. A defender is on her fast and she taps it out to Micah then runs past the defender for a perfect wall pass and shoots, but the goalie dives and saves it from the lower right-hand corner and half the crowd cheers and half groans.

"Great work!" Grandma yells.

Aunt Tam is clapping and saying, "Keep the pressure on!"

I'm looking at the doors of the school waiting for Maximilian to walk out with his notebook and his goofy smile and wave to me but when the door doesn't open I start wondering if he got caught thinking about the court date and his mom and if he's stuck and head-shaky and needs help and there's no one there to start counting *eight, sixteen . . .*

I'm about to raise my hand for Tess to sub in so I can go check, but their goalie punts the ball right to me. I dead trap it and look up. Their captain, number ten, is closing in fast so I quick fake right and take the ball left and around her. I hear A clapping for the ball and pointing and her dad is jumping up and cheering, "Great run, A!" and I send it to her on the left wing and charge toward goal. She tries to pass it to Cara, but it's cut off by a defender and they're coming back down the field.

"Recover!" A's mom calls, and I wish the ball would go out-of-bounds so I could raise my hand and get out of the game and go find Maximilian.

When I run past our bench I ask again, "Where's Maximilian?" Tess puts her arms out like she doesn't know. She starts looking around, and Nelle's mom points down the field where Quinn is containing the other team's forward and Georgia is rushing to help. But I can't get back in time and they have a wide-open midfielder who gets the ball and has space for a shot and it flies past Fern in goal.

They go wild and rush the scorer and all run together

back to their side of the field while the crowd settles and Grandma Bea is clapping and saying, "It's OK, team! You got this!"

I run to the bench and ask if I can come out to look for Maximilian. "He said he was going to the bathroom. I don't know where he is."

Tess says she'll go but then Jamie says she needs a sub and the referee is whistling and telling us to line up and Tess is running out to do the kickoff with Cara and Micah and I'm stuck on the field.

Bryce and Wendell are making their way toward the bench and asking what's wrong and Bryce says he'll go check and I'm thinking that might be the worst idea ever but then I remember how he worked with us today in math class and how he hasn't laughed along with Konny and Morris since they wore sports bras and lipstick and tripped and giggled down the hall.

"Your team needs you," he says. Then he looks right at me. "I got this."

The whistle blows and Bryce runs off and around the field and through the big doors on the side of the school and Tess taps the ball to Micah, who sends it up to Cara, and I make my feet follow them.

We go back and forth three times. Cece misses a shot wide, Fern saves a shot on goal, their defender steals the ball from Georgia and sends us all recovering back quickly and my lungs and legs are burning from all the running. But I'm also watching the double doors.

They don't open.

Instead, as Nelle clears a ball from defense and Cece runs to track it down, I hear sirens. They get louder and closer and they turn into the drive for our school, and right up to the loop where the buses sit.

The whistle blows and it's halftime, and the other team is jogging off the field to their bench, but I'm running toward the school. And I'm not thinking about a single other thing except that deep down ache in my belly and how it hurts worse every time my heart beats *team-team*. I pull open the heavy doors and run, my cleats clicking against the floor, toward the boys' locker room. I hear voices but I'm breathing too hard to make out what they're saying and I can't stop until I get there and see Bryce and Kenny and Morris all standing back.

Watching Maximilian scream.

Principal Meesley is there trying to calm him down but he's doing it all wrong and it's making it worse.

There is blood from a cut on Maximilian's ear, and he's clutching his backpack with a fist so tight his knuckles are white. The EMT and paramedic are telling Maximilian that he's OK, they're here to help him, and I wish it were my mom who drove the ambulance, because then maybe she'd let me help. "Eight! Sixteen!

Twenty-four! Squeeze next to his thumb!" I don't realize I'm screaming until the paramedic asks me to quiet
down and move back. And I know from my mom that
you're not supposed to yell when someone is out of control but I just can't help it and I want everyone to clear
out so I can go in.

Maximilian is grabbing his ear with his other hand
and then his hair and shaking his head hard left and
right and choking down breaths. The EMT stands up
and moves us all into the closest classroom, Mr. Henny's,
while the paramedic sits down quietly on the floor with
Maximilian and models deep inhales and loud exhales.

The EMT looks at me and Kenny and Morris and
Bryce and Principal Meesley and says it'll help Maximilian if we all give him space for a few moments until
he catches his breath, but I hate that he's trying to tell
me about my best friend.

I hear other voices in the hall now. Nelle and A and
Cara and Aunt Tam. They're calling for Maximilian and
me. The EMT tells us to stay put and he'll be back to get
us when it's safe for Maximilian. The door clicks and he
rushes to clear the halls, the voices of my teammates
fading back toward the double doors and outside.

"This is all so unfortunate," Principal Meesley says
and he actually looks sad when he says it.

Maximilian's screams are getting softer but I can't

see him from the skinny window on the classroom door so I don't know what's happening or if they've contacted his grandparents or if he's asking for me.

Principal Meesley rubs his forehead then asks Kenny and Morris, "What happened?"

They both shrug.

Then I look straight at them. "What. Happened?"

Kenny looks at Morris and Morris looks back. "We were joking around. Then he just freaked out."

"Yeah," Morris says. "It was out of nowhere."

Principal Meesley starts to say, "I'm sure he'll be OK. I'm sure it's a big misunderstanding."

"No," I say. "It's not. You all have known Maximilian since second grade. It's not a misunderstanding."

I think I hear the crinkling of Maximilian's breath into a paper bag in the hallway. The paramedic's voice is calm.

Bryce is staring at our number line posters on Mr. Henny's wall and for a second I think he's counting down, maybe even by eights, because his eyes get a little watery and he starts to breathe harder like he can't stay calm either.

I look at Kenny and Morris again. "What. Did. You. Do?" I punch each word straight at their lying little faces.

"Nothing. He just overreacted."

"No," Bryce says. He doesn't take his eyes from the

number line posters and his voice is kind of shaky, but he says, "When I got here I heard Kenny saying, *You're going to be late for your game with the* girls. *Better run.*"

"Is that true?" Principal Meesley asks Kenny and Morris.

But I don't care what they have to say, so I get my punches ready. "Why. Is. He. Bleeding?"

"He slipped," Morris says.

"He's like the clumsiest kid in the grade. Everyone knows that," Kenny adds.

Bryce breaks his trance from the number line and looks at Principal Meesley because Bryce is not a clinging molecule. "They were bullying him," he says. "Telling him he was in the wrong bathroom and asking him if he was changing into his team uniform so he could prance across the field with the rest of the girls."

Then I can't believe it but Kenny's eyes get a little watery, but he blinks fast and says, "He was acting like a scaredy-cat, so whatever, yeah, I called him a girl."

I glare at Principal Meesley and he lowers his eyes. My hands clench into fists.

"Maximilian tried to get by them but they weren't moving and he got tripped up," Bryce continues. "He fell into the lockers. He must have cut his ear then."

Principal Meesley shakes his head. He looks serious. "That's unacceptable," he says. And I'm thinking two things. One, *Finally.* Kenny and Morris have been deserving trouble for a long time. And two, *Hypocrite.* I've heard Meesley with my own two ears call Kenny and Wyatt scaredy-cat girls for shying off the ball at practice.

Then he says, "It's unacceptable to taunt someone like that, and call them a girl."

And I don't even have time to bite my tongue in the back of my mouth because I'm thinking of Grandma Bea, and Mom, and A, and Leslie Burke from *Bridge to Terabithia*, and little Val working on her lungs in the hospital, and so I say, right to water-bug Meesley, "That is some serious bullsharky."

"Excuse me?"

"I said that is some serious bullsharky."

He wrinkles his brow and says, "You need to mind your tongue."

So I do. I mind my tongue by making sure it's not caught between my teeth and I say, "It's terrible what they did, but you're making it sound like the worst part of it all is being called a girl. And being a girl isn't bad. We're not little. Or less. Or quitters. We're actually pretty badass."

He wrinkles his brow again when I say that word, but I don't care.

"I didn't say that girls were less . . ." he starts.

But there's a knock at the door and the EMT comes

in and explains that they're taking Maximilian to the hospital for a checkup. He had a minor injury to the ear and a pretty severe panic attack. Then he nods to Bryce and thanks him for calling. "You were right. He needed help."

Then Officer Berkley from the police station in town comes in and asks to see Principal Meesley and Kenny and Morris in the office.

Now it's Kenny and Morris who look like scaredy-cats, and so does Principal Meesley. And I'm thinking it serves them right.

Bryce says he'll go too. "I saw most of what happened." Officer Berkley nods and says that would be helpful.

As we file out the door, I see Maximilian walking slowly down the hall with the paramedic. He's still clutching his backpack. The EMT jogs to catch up and Principal Meesley looks at me and says, "I didn't say that being a girl was less. I didn't say that." And I almost feel bad for him because it looks like he believes that's true.

Then he follows Officer Berkley to the office and I go the other way back toward the double doors and the field. I don't know how long I've been inside or if the game is still going on and if we're still losing 0–1, but before I push open the doors, I call for Principal Meesley and he turns back.

"You did say it. You've been saying it all season. And we have evidence."

The game is still going and when I get to the bench Grandma Bea fills me in. We're tied 1–1 with five minutes left. I fill Grandma Bea in too, about Maximilian, and she covers her mouth and shakes her head.

Quinn is taking a turn in goal and A has the ball in the midfield. Her pass to Cara is cut off and knocked out-of-bounds and Emmie's raising her hand for a sub.

I run in and give her a high five and Cece throws the ball up the line to Micah. Georgia runs close to me and asks about Maximilian. I fill her in then she tells Quinn. The word about what happened is getting around the field and the sideline too. I can tell because people keep shaking their heads and covering their mouths.

Then Micah's taking the ball to the corner and Jamie and A are running in for a cross, but the defender steals the ball and passes it through to their midfielder captain number ten. I'm trying to contain her, but she's fast and strong and knows how to do step-over-scissor fakes too. I know I have Georgia back and Nelle, but they're trying to mark the forwards who are making runs toward our goal.

Then she rolls the ball to her left foot and passes it through Fern and Nelle to their forward, who gets away from Georgia and barely gets a foot on it, but the ball slides in past Quinn in goal. We're down 2–1.

They run in to celebrate and Quinn gets the ball from the back of the net and slams it hard against the ground.

We run to her and tell her it's OK, that their whole team scored on our whole team and being a goalie is hard. "They're really good," I tell everyone. "And so are we."

"Just keep playing our best," A says.

Then I see Aunt Tam pointing over our heads to the parking lot and Wendell stands up from the bench and A's mom too. Maximilian is walking out with the EMT and the paramedic, and his grandparents are pulling in behind the ambulance. His grandma rushes out of the passenger side as soon as their car stops.

Maximilian has an oxygen mask on his mouth now. His shoulders are still heaving hard and the EMT is holding gauze over his ear, but he looks over to the field and waves. Then he stops and puts one finger up to the non-gauzy side of his head, his bull horn. And he paws and kicks the sidewalk with his sneaker. Charge.

We all do it back, kick our cleats like hooves in the grass, and grunt like bulls ready to stampede, and I can see Maximilian smile before they help him and his grandma into the back of the ambulance.

* * *

There are two minutes left in the game and we don't score.

We don't win.

The end-of-game whistle blows and the other team screams and jumps and my shoulders sink and my heart aches a beat.

But then I hear Grandma Bea.

"Whoo-hooooooo!" and she's rushing the field with Aunt Tam and A's mom and our hundred other coaches, who have supervised practices, filled our bench, and crowded our sideline every game. They pull us into our last huddle of the season and tell us how proud they are of us. How far we've come, together. And I can feel my shoulders rise back up. There are twenty-two hands in our end-of-season *team* cheer. I know because I counted. For Maximilian. So we can add it to our team notebook.

After our cheer Cameron and Tucker come over to the bench and put their arms around my shoulders, and all the kids from our school say *good job* and give high fives.

Then I see A's dad waiting to give her a big hug. At first she just kind of lets him hug her and he does and then he does again and says, "This is quite a team you girls have made." He pinches her earlobe and smiles and that feels like maybe it's their thing. Like *I love you all the way up to the Care Bears* or how Mom kisses me on the forehead. Like a tiny slice of their in-between time and I wasn't supposed to be in on it. "I'm proud of you," he tells her.

He says he has a flight out of Burlington to catch but he'll be back soon, for longer, and he hugs her one more time and I'm trying not to watch because it's none of my business, but I see A hug him back, really squeeze him hard.

24

I WAKE UP NEXT to Grandma Bea and before I can rub the sleep out of my eyes I know she's holding up three fingers.

Grandma Bea's threes feel hard this morning. I want to say Mom and Grandma and Aunt Tam and Maximilian because they've been with me forever and Val because my heart loves her so much already and Wendell because even though he has a tiny blue porcelain container stuffed away, and a deep down achy spot in his gut, he still makes my mom laugh and gets all snorty-Valentine-lovey about her and me and that feels more than pretty good. And I want to say Cameron and Tucker because they're funny and gentle and never act like it's weird to live with me. And Bryce. Because he's strong enough to break a bond of clinging little molecules. And A, because we're tougher together. And Cece and Emmie and Quinn and everyone for playing and standing up and moving together. And Ms. Blaise and Ms. Kravitz . . .

"Come on. Three." Grandma nudges me.

We're face-to-face on my pillow and I'm looking right into her green eyes. Eyes that look like Mom's and mine, and I hold up one finger. Then I make the sign for *team* with a big, exaggerated circle of my fists like I'm trying to hold everyone inside it.

Grandma Bea smiles and kisses me on my forehead. "I guess one will do for today," she says. "Because things won't always go exactly the same way forever."

"What's your one?" I ask.

"M&M's for breakfast," she says. "Because *some* things don't ever change."

Kenny and Morris have in-school suspension with Ms. Landry, but Maximilian is back in class today and he has two apology letters in his hand, one from Kenny and one from Morris. I bet Principal Meesley or Officer Berkley made them write those. Bryce told me last night that when they all went back to the office after the Maximilian incident, Officer Berkley explained to Kenny and Morris that what they did was illegal, and then gave Principal Meesley a whole lecture about combating bullying in his school.

Maximilian lets me read the apology letters and they're both different so I know they didn't just copy, and they actually sound pretty real. Like maybe they really are sorry and they're ready to give up on being mean and they'll stop and think for a minute before they do something as stupid as dress up like the girls' team or bother Maximilian again. Maybe they'll even grow more than three brain cells.

I put my two hands on the outsides of Maximilian's shoulders and he puts his hands on mine too.

"I'm glad you're OK," I say.

He nods and walks to the back of the classroom. Then he puts his hands on the outsides of Bryce's shoulders and says, "Thanks."

Bryce laughs a little, but not a laugh-at-you kind of laugh, a this-is-kind-of-weird-but-I'm-going-with-it kind of laugh and he says, "No problem, Maximilian."

Maximilian didn't need any stitches for his ear, but it's covered with a Band-Aid and he had to stay in the hospital for two hours so the doctors could help him regulate his breathing.

He reaches into his backpack, the one he clutched in his fist and held on to while Kenny and Morris were bullying him, and he pulls out the team notebook.

When he slides it over to me I say, "You're the best manager ever."

He smiles. "I know."

Ms. Blaise is asking us to get out our pencils and notebooks so we can work on our claim and evidence paragraphs.

I'm digging in my backpack when my hand finds the balled-up piece of paper from our first practice. The notes I ripped out and threw across my room, the notes Maximilian copied back into the first page of the notebook to keep, Principal Meesley's notes in Maximilian's shaky, scared handwriting.

I flatten it out on my table and start crossing out Principal Meesley's words and making some claims of my own.

#21 Quinn: ~~no first touch~~ Steady

#6 Emmie: ~~fast start, no stamina~~ Confident

#12 Georgia: ~~agreeable, could play anywhere~~ Kind

#4 Tess: ~~clumsy~~ Fearless

#16 Micah: ~~weak shot~~ Dependable

#10 Cece: ~~surprisingly quick, hard to coach?~~ Independent

#13 Nelle: ~~out of shape, sensitive~~ Supportive

#9 A: ~~skills, ego~~ Good leader

#8 Fern: ~~no power~~ Consistent

#15 Cara: ~~no control~~ Determined
#18 Jamie: ~~slow~~ Thoughtful
#1 Bea: ~~goalie, attitude~~ Team player
Maximilian: ~~Weak~~ Brave

Cece looks over my shoulder and smiles and signs *Thank you* and adds some words to the list then passes it along to Georgia and A.

And when Ms. Blaise comes to visit our table to ask if she can help us put the final touches on our paragraphs, I show her my notebook page with a whole paragraph about how my soccer team is persistent.

"I'm done with that assignment," I say. But I tell her we have a whole bunch of evidence we've been collecting about a different belief we have. A belief that next year we should have a new coach, a coach who won't wish we'd be quitters, or think we're worth a day less than the boys.

I hand her the notebook and she turns to the first page. I know the words she's reading. *Clumsy, attitude . . . Boys get new uniforms, girls can fundraise if they want . . . You'll quit before the first game . . . You want to take another day from the boys? . . . All in good fun . . . Scaredy-cats! If you want to win games you can't shy off the ball like a couple of little girls.* All the notes are dated and organized and I can see Ms. Blaise's lip quiver before she clamps her teeth down hard.

"I'm so sorry," she says. She looks right in my eyes and then in Cece's and A's and everyone's. Not just our team and not even just the girls. She holds up the notebook and says to all of us, "I'm so sorry that you have been receiving these messages."

And I can tell that's not the last thing she has to say about that.

A bunch of us stay in for recess to make a plan with Ms. Blaise and Ms. Kravitz. A plan to use our evidence, to use our voices, to use our teamwork to get a new coach for next season. We're writing down our claims and using the examples to create paragraphs that we'll give to Principal Meesley. Before the period ends, a few of us share:

A's claim: The girls' team could go further with a better coach.
Cece's claim: It didn't feel like Principal Meesley was on our team.
My claim: We deserve better.

And when the bell rings and we start packing up I hear Ms. Kravitz say something to Ms. Blaise about how he shouldn't be a boys' coach either, or a principal for that matter.

291

She leans into Ms. Blaise and whispers, "I'm all about people learning and growing, but he needs his feet held to the fire."

And I swear they give each other a secret little teacher fist bump.

On the way to the bus, I see Principal Meesley's office door open. It's never open so I look in and accidentally catch his eye. I start walking faster but I hear his voice. "Embers!"

At first I pretend I don't hear but he says it again and he even stands up and comes out in the hallway. "Embers! A minute?"

I tell A and Bryce to save me a seat on the bus and head back toward his office. He gestures for me to step in and I see on his round table a bunch of books about *Combating Bullying in Your School* and *Bias* and *Restorative Justice*. I think Officer Berkley gave those to him after the incident with Maximilian.

"I—I really didn't mean to say that girls are less."

"But you did."

He nods his head like he knows and I'm thinking that's a start. A tiny start. The tiniest.

As soon as the bus stops on Evergreen Road I pop up from my seat, hustle to the front, jump, and clear the three steps to the street. Bryce is right behind me and we dead sprint, our backpacks flying back and forth on our shoulders, all the way home. Then we stop quick and tiptoe toward the door in the garage and creak it open.

"Come in already!" Mom calls, so we pull off our shoes and drop our bags and find her on the couch. Val is sleeping on Mom, so we walk over quietly and bend down to look at her little baby face. I can hear the breath in her nose. Her cheek is pressed into Mom's chest, and she has one little fist pulled up next to her face.

Wendell's making tea in the kitchen and I can see Cameron and Tucker out the window, running across the front yard from the high school bus stop. They inch the door open just like we did and Mom calls for them to get in here already too and Val doesn't even budge, she just keeps breathing through that little nose. Her whole body rises up and down with each one of Mom's breaths, like Mom's lungs are teaching hers just what to do.

Then we're all there. Wendell and Cameron and Tucker and Bryce and Dodger and Roscoe and Fred and we're all making a little circle, the sign for *team*, the sign for *family*, around baby Val, just watching her breathe.

And I'll tell you one thing. It feels like a win.

ACKNOWLEDGMENTS

My nana really did wake my mom up in the mornings with "three things you're grateful for, big or small." The sentiment, if not the daily tradition, was handed down to me and I often find myself returning to those "threes." During the writing of this book I have had so much to be grateful for. So here I am, with a story I love, doing my own nana's "threes."

One, I am grateful for the strong circle of women I was born into, and the strong circles of women I have linked arms with along the way, to call team. My nana, my grandma, and my mom are the source of my strength, and I have been so blessed with aunts and "aunts" and cousins and "sisters" and teammates and roommates and classmates and friends who lift me up.

Special thanks to Lauren Catherwood-Ginn, Stephanie Douglas, Briana Herbert, Jess McFarlane, Jennifer Ochoa, Candas Pinar, Jess Rothenberg, Adriana Saipe, and my Carleton 7 for being ever-present through the writing of this book, and always. Your friendship and humor brighten me.

Two, the incredible book-creating team I have. My soccer-loving agent, Stephen Barbara, cheered Bea from the beginning and has a wonderful way of reminding me, through each book, that *I got this*. I continue to be incredibly honored to work with my editor, Erica Sussman. Her succinct, thoughtful editorial comments made this book tighter and stronger, and her succinct, hilarious friendship-check-in emails make me laugh out loud. She has made me a smarter writer and I'm just so grateful for the footprints she left on Bea's story. I'm also grateful for the whole team at HarperCollins, who had a hand in making this book what it is. Thank you for all the care you have taken, Jessica Berg, Veronica Ambrose, Gwen Morton, Louisa Currigan, Chris Kwon, Alison Donalty, Anne Dye, Aubrey Churchward, Rebecca McGuire, and Patty Rosati.

And three, the family I have at home. I did the revisions and edits for this book while people all over the world were staying home, sheltering-in, trying to flatten the curve of the Covid-19 outbreak. Kamahnie, all the things we teach our kids—how to take turns, act with kindness, think of others, share, be present, say yes to adventure and yes to getting cozy-cozy with a book—are the things I love in you. You are an excellent co-captain. Thank you for making this an adventure, for sharing, and taking turns, and being present. And I'll tell you one thing. Miles and Paige, my greatest joy has been watching the two of you become teammates.